MINDWORM

BY

DAVID POLLARD

for Joe and Jess
with thanks
David Pollard
1/8/2020

DEDICATION

For my son James, his wife Hayley

And my two lovely grandchildren Imogen and George

ISBN: 9798638307943

BY THE SAME AUTHOR

ALSO PUBLISHED BY AMAZON

NOVELS

The Alienation of Ludovic Weiss

SHORT STORY COLLECTIONS

His Cat and Other Strange Tales

PLAYS PUBLISHED BY LAZYBEE SCRIPTS (www.lazybee.com)

Can Malone Die?
Aspects of a Betrayal
Clause Fourteen
Illusion/Delusion
Nobbo

CHAPTER ONE

What you are never told about road trips is that most of the roads are long and tedious and that the trip is lonely and gives you too much time to think. But then I wasn't on a road trip.

I was certainly sick of this desert highway. I was tired of the ribbon of two-lane blacktop that stretched to infinity beyond the beams of the headlights just as it had stretched under the sunlight for hours before. I was tired of the inane talk of the disc-jockeys punctuating the same dozen or so records by the same dozen or so bands. Their voices and the tunes morphed into one another as station succeeded station; the bland yielding the airwaves to the bland.

I wanted company. I wanted to hear the babble and froth of real conversations. I wanted to talk to another human being and to smell their warmth.

I had been on the road for seven days now. A week of keeping low and avoiding places that were too small and where I would be an obvious stranger; an arrival worthy of remark. I'd kept an eye on the newspapers and the local television wherever I had stopped. Sometimes, when no favourable location offered I had simply pulled the car off the road and slumped exhausted behind the wheel for a couple of hours of fitful sleep before the rising sun called me back onto the road.

I seemed to have a natural talent for making myself invisible, for merging into the background. When I thought about it and I had plenty of time to think in that week on the road, it was playing into a lifetime predilection. I'd always been a solitary, an outsider, preferring my own company, avoiding crowds, avoiding the need to keep up my end of a conversation.

Lights twinkling in the desert darkness came up on the horizon and a few miles later I crossed into the town. It was nothing much, just a couple of motels by the roadside and a deserted main street, the shops closed and shuttered for the night, leading away to where the desert started once more. Further out in the darkness a collection of one storey houses, a few with lights still burning in the windows, told the tale of a population tucked up snug for the night.

I cruised slowly down Main Street looking for a sign of life. I found it right at the end just where the blackness gathered. Over on the left a bar - Tom's Place - a few pickup trucks parked around the door and a couple of loungers in the warm night, sipping their beer from the bottles, propping up the wall by the half-opened door. On the other side of the street was what I was really looking for.

The cafe shone out like a beacon, lights blazing out of the plate glass windows into the night. Inside was like a scene from one of Hopper's paintings - you know the one, it's called 'Nighthawks'. A cop hunched over a cup as he sat at the counter. A couple held hands over the table in a booth set right at the back of the room. Two women sat at separate tables, one in the window, and the other over by the door while two men in business suits eyed them from the safety of the booth they shared.

I stepped out of the air-conditioned chill of the car and into the syrupy warmth of a desert night.

When I entered the room the hum of conversation stopped for just a moment as I became for that brief instant of time a creature worthy of notice. I found myself a seat in a booth from where I could see the door and the murmur of human activity resumed and embraced me.

I picked up a wrinkled and well-thumbed copy of a newspaper. At least it was the edition for that day. A glance at the front page told me that I was still not newsworthy. No pictures of my face, no headlines, no pleas from the police for public cooperation. I let myself relax and glanced at the inside of the paper, not focussing, and let my attention drift to an awareness of the other occupants of the cafe.

The cop continued to brood into his cup. He was having a bad day and he just wanted to get home. The couple in the booth in back wanted to be anywhere else, so long as they could be alone. The two guys speculated anxiously which of the two women offered the better prospect and which of them had the best chance. The two women had completely other things on their mind.

I sensed her beside me before she spoke and turned my eyes up to meet her unengaged glance.

'Hi - how're you this evening? What can I get for you?'

The pin on her gingham overall said she was called Abby.

'Well I'm tired and I'm hungry - so what's good?'

‘The chilli’s the special today. Just like it is every day’

‘I’ll take the chilli then’

‘If you want the truth the chilli is never that special. Try the steak fried chicken. At least that gets cooked up fresh. Probably won’t poison you either.’

‘I’ll be guided by you. Thanks for the tip...Abby.’

‘No big deal. You want coffee?’

‘Sure’

The food arrived and I ate slowly, satisfying my immediate hunger while the thoughts around me in the room tickled another appetite.

The cop got himself to his feet and headed heavily for the door on his way home to an unsympathetic welcome. As he passed my booth he gave me hardly a glance and was soon swallowed up by the night. The couple in back left right after the cop to seek the solitude they craved. Soon enough there was only me and Abby and the short-order cook in the place. Cookie started to make noisy preparations for closing up. I finished my food and slugged back a last dreg from my cup.

'Can I get you anything else?' Abby was beside me even before the coffee cup chinked back on the saucer.

'No, thanks, that's fine.' She handed me the check and I forked over some currency.

'Everything OK?'

'Fine. I'm not hungry anymore but I'm bushed. Maybe you can help me out. Which one of those motels back along the street would be my best choice?'

She looked me over coolly. I noticed she had green eyes and auburn hair caught up under a cute waitress cap that matched her overall. Her creamy skin was lightly freckled as if she'd been dusted with cinnamon.

'You look to me like you could use a little conversation and some company before you turn in. Been on the road a long time?'

'A few days. But, yeah, you're right; it does get kind of lonely on the road.'

'I'm off now -just as soon as Clarence finishes up. Wait for me. I usually stop by Tom's for a drink after my shift. Come and have one with me and we can figure out where you can get a bed for the night.'

She was back in a couple of minutes, the gingham overall replaced by a tee-shirt and blue jeans, her hair shaken out and shiny as it cascaded over her shoulders. It was certainly no hardship to follow her across the street and through the door of Tom's Place.

The bar-room was dark and crowded with bodies. The buzz of conversation never checked as we slipped into the room. Above the chatter waves of thought drifted over to me. It was warm and comfortable and appetising. Abby led and we threaded our way through the crowd and we took possession of an empty booth.

The first beer slipped down pleasantly, long and cool, while we exchanged names and pleasantries. A second round appeared almost without my knowing it. I was starting to relax and to enjoy myself, almost forgetting what had brought me here. Abby soon jerked me back to alertness, forcing my guard back into position.

'So what are you doing way out here?'

I was ready for this. I'd spent many of the long hours alone figuring out my story for anyone who might ask. Even so the words didn't slip out easily and I hoped the girl hadn't remarked any special reticence in my tone.

'Well, it's a sort of vacation. I found I had some time on my hands and no particular plans. So I hopped in the car and set out to see this great country of ours.'

'Not the usual tourist route through here. Are you lost?'

'No, just had no plans, no special direction. And I guess I had other things on my mind.'

'Uh huh. That'll do it'

'Yeah. Just got in the car and started heading west.'

'Do you want to talk about it?'

'Uh?'

'Whatever was on your mind?'

This was starting to get out of hand. I hesitated for longer than was seemly.

'It's OK if you don't...'

'Well, you know I said I had some time on my hands. It all came as something of a surprise. I got laid off you see.'

'What do you do? Or what did you do?'

This was getting complicated and maybe she'd get too close to the truth. Maybe she knew something already. Maybe she was guessing at who I was already. She sipped her beer and smiled a disarming, naive smile. No, she couldn't know. I hedged.

'What do you think I did?'

'You look like a college professor to me or maybe a librarian. I guess it's the tweed jacket and the horn-rimmed glasses. Oh yeah, and that cute little moustache'

She was smart or maybe I was just obviously what I was. No point denying but I could see a way of getting myself off the hook of interrogation.

'You're quite the observer. You've summed me up in one shot. Librarian - that's me. But what about you? This town doesn't look like the place to harbour someone with your intelligence.'

'Uh, uh. You're wrong there. Home town girl that's me. Born and raised right around the corner.'

'But you've plans,' I pushed, 'going to get out one day...'

'Sure. Now Mom and Pop have passed on there's nothing to keep me here.'

I chugged back my beer and made a big show of kneading sleepy eyes.

'Well, thanks for your company, Abby. But now I'm really all in. Can you point me to the best of those two motels?'

'I think we can do better than that for you. Why not come on home with me. Plenty of room. Call it country hospitality.'

'Aren't you taking a chance here? I could be anyone.'

'You look pretty harmless to me. I'm a pretty good judge. You're OK. Now stop gabbing and come with me.'

I wasn't in a mood to argue and the invitation was very attractive. Although I was wary I was enjoying myself. I decided to let fate take its course. There seemed no point arguing anyway as Abby grabbed my hand and almost heaved me out of the place.

Abby led me along a side street and up to a single storey house that was all in darkness.

'This was Mom and Pop's place. And you're right about me too. As soon as I sell up I'm out of here. First step college in Corpus Christi, then the world.'

She led me through the darkened lounge, past the kitchen and into a bedroom.

'This should be OK for you...'

I agreed that, indeed, I should be very comfortable.

'Shower's right through there. You probably want to freshen up. I'll be right back.'

It was a real relief to shuck off my road soiled clothes and step into the shower. It felt good to let the warm water cascade over my body, easing the kinks in my muscles, sloughing off the film of desert dust.

Over the trickle and splash of the water I heard the shower stall door click open and shut again. A hand reached over and plucked the soap from my grasp. Firm hands lathered my shoulders and worked down to the small of my back easing the tensions they found there. She turned me to face her. The effect was instantaneous and very obvious.

'Looks like we've both got an itch that needs attending to,' she smiled and tossed me a towel.

Back in the bedroom she lay down and drew me down beside her. It felt good to be close to another human being. She smelt clean and fresh. Her skin was soft and smooth against me.

With release, exhaustion claimed me. I felt warm and secure, nothing threatened me. I felt Abby's arms and legs twine about me drawing me to her softness. I let myself drift off into an ink black and dreamless sleep.

When I woke up the noonday sun was streaming through the slats of the blind, flooding the room with light and casting shadows over the bed. Abby lay beside me tangled in the sheets and still fast asleep.

I felt the hunger inside me, nagging at my insides. Where would be the harm? I looked at

Abby's sleeping form. She grunted in her sleep and rolled onto her back. I can't say I made up my mind to yield to the urging inside me, I simply gave in to it.

It only took a moment to enter her. She was dreaming. To someone like me, with my particular needs, dreams are rare and delicious appetisers. Abby's was light and tempting, made of hopes, the future and glorious anticipations not marred at all by fears and suppressed experiences.

I'd promised myself just to taste, just to take the merest taste, but once begun I supped with the relish and urgency of a starving man. Like all good appetisers Abby's dreams simply left me wanting more and now I could not restrain myself. I gorged on her unconscious in an orgy of feeding, tapping the vital energy of her experiences and memories, devouring her emotions. When I had sated myself I withdrew and curled myself on her breast and slept once more.

Much later I came awake again with a start. The day was waning now and shadows were beginning to lengthen. Abby's naked form was cold beneath me and I knew what I had done.

I sat on the edge of the bed and hugged myself. I began to shudder uncontrollably as the horror of what I am capable of doing enveloped me. Tears stung my eyes and coursed down my face. She had been a delight, young, full of promise and she had shown me kindness. And I had destroyed her. In a few moments of uncontrolled frenzy I had stolen the life force from this wonder of creation.

Then the survival imperative grasped me and I realised that what I had done was far more terrible than simply despatching another human being. I had left a sign. A sign that he could not mistake. I knew he'd be watching for it and this - Abby's death, the discovery of a young woman dead without a mark on her sweet creamy flesh - would bring him here. Then he would know that I had been here. He would know where I was running and would pick up my trail.

Panic turned rapidly to calculation. I guessed that Abby's shift at the cafe wouldn't start until early evening and if she didn't turn up for work no-one would come looking. I probably had maybe twenty-four hours before anyone might discover the body. I knew for a fact there was no boyfriend who might come calling and no family to wonder where she might be. I knew I could proceed calmly so I showered and dressed. I helped myself to food and a couple of cold beers and some sodas from the refrigerator so that I could avoid stopping for supplies for several hundred miles on my route away from here.

I looked at Abby's dead body lying among the crumpled bed sheets. I couldn't leave her like that. It wouldn't be decent. I owed her at least a vestige of respect. Carefully I arranged her on the bed and laid her head on a pillow. When I had finished she looked like she was peacefully asleep. I drew a sheet over her and covered her face.

I gave Abby's dead form one last glance and let myself out.

The car was just where I had left it. I checked for parking violation notices on the windscreen and was relieved to find that the vehicle seemed to have escaped any official scrutiny. I drove carefully down to the town's gas station and filled the tank.

Back out on the highway I put in some more calculation. When he saw my sign my pursuer would see that I had been heading west ever since I had started to run. Would he figure that I'd just keep running in the same direction? He would surely realise that I would know that Abby's death would bring him running and that I'd try to throw him off the scent. It was useless to try to double guess him. I was just succeeding in tying myself into ever more intricate knots. An intersection loomed and on the spur of the moment I made up my mind to travel south.

CHAPTER TWO

I am not a killer. Let me make that clear. The anguish and self-loathing I felt at the death of Abby at my hands was beyond describing. I hated that the frenzy of my appetite had been her instrument of destruction.

It was an irony that my outward appearance had convinced her that I was harmless. How effectively had a worn tweed jacket and thick black – framed glasses hidden the darkness that lurked inside me.

I never knew my natural parents. By the time I was old enough to form memories of them they had disappeared from my life. No one ever explained what had happened to them and I never thought to ask. Growing up I made up stories about them for myself and to explain their absence from my life. As I grew to maturity I gave that up and simply accepted that they were not there.

I was brought up by an aunt and uncle. At least that's what everybody, myself included, believed. It was a given fact that was never questioned. They were good to me and my childhood was perfectly normal and void of all but the usual traumas of growing up. I didn't form friendships and there were just a few, brief, adolescent encounters with girls. I was bookish, which seemed to please my aunt and uncle. I worked hard at school and gave little trouble.

I must have been born to be a librarian. As soon as I walked into the library at my small town New England college I felt that I was meant to be there. The smell of polish and wood, of dust and paper, enveloped me like a mother folding a child to her breast. It wasn't just that though. There was something else in the stillness. It was the latency of knowledge and experience contained between the leather and cardboard jackets. I was thirsty, even then, for what the books contained. It was as if each volume was reaching out to me and aching to be devoured.

It was inevitable that, my degree completed, I should stay on and take the librarian's qualification. It was also inevitable, having formed a bond with the Chief Librarian during my college years that I should be appointed as one of his assistants. Where else would I want to be? What else could I want to be? You may think of me as unambitious, but then what is ambition but seeking after unfulfilled desires? I had everything I wanted so what was there to strive for? The library was not my second home; it was where I preferred to be. The small apartment I acquired was just a short walk from the college campus and my employment and it was simply a place to sleep and store the essentials of my life. Most of my waking hours were spent in the library.

Tom Petersen, the Chief Librarian, had become more than just a valued colleague and supervisor. We shared a common enthusiasm. We were not employer and employee but co-conspirators, sharing a common love and vision for the resource entrusted to us. So you see my working life was harmonious to say the least. I had a good salary, comfortable lodging and a good friend. What more could there be?

If the truth were known, Tom Petersen and his wife became my surrogate parents. I relied on them for guidance and for some warmth in what was an essentially lonely and isolated life.

If I had an ambition it was simply to be my mentor Petersen's successor and to carry on the work he had started. I was in no hurry. That is an essential fact for you to grasp. Petersen was not in my way and to some extent I rather hoped that he would never disappear from my life.

My boss was a softly spoken bear of a man. He moved slowly and deliberately. In any crisis he was a centre of calm and control. Above all he shared my passion for the proximity of books and that drew me to him initially and kept our relationship close. Naturally, over the course of years, we disagreed but it was always at the level of calm conversation; voices were never raised. Until that afternoon I had never known him to show anger but when he returned from his meeting and slammed the door of his office shut behind him he was a pent up ball of rage.

I had no idea what triggered this extreme show of emotion. I could only guess that it was something that had taken place during the meeting that threatened the library. I sat outside Petersen's office for a while listening to the commotion within and debating whether or not to intrude. Eventually the noise of pacing and the slamming of books and files on desktop abated and was replaced by an uncomfortable silence and I dared to enter.

Petersen was sprawled in his chair behind his desk. He looked up at me but he was not seeing me, he was not registering my presence. His gaze bored through me. His face was crimson and his eyes bulged as sweat poured off his forehead. It was a heart attack for sure and I made to loosen his collar.

Then it happened. An intense flush of heat suffused my body and my vision clouded. I was pitched forward, not pushed but drawn into a whirlpool of movement. I put out my hands to grasp something, anything solid, but I was tumbling, tumbling into a void. There was a rushing of noise, high and low notes combined and then everything became still.

I was in a neutral space. There were no walls and everything as far as I could see was a uniform milky grey. Except that is for the fragment of redness that was in front of me. It was an insubstantial mist and I passed through it and into a meadow beyond. The grey was now replaced by intense green and blue light. At the edge of the meadow I could just make out the form of a woman, seated and bent over a book, reading intently.

I started to move towards her but with every step she seemed to recede further into the distance. Then the sensations began to crowd in on me; disembodied voices, familiar sounds and unfamiliar harmonies. In a state of turmoil I experienced a flood of emotions; love, hate, violence and passion. There was experience too and knowledge hard won.

Like an infant animal presented to the teat I knew what to do. I fed. Hungrily I consumed everything that whirled around me. It was a frenzy of feeding on a food I knew instinctively I had craved for my entire existence.

Then, as suddenly as it had begun it was finished. I felt myself ejected into the void and came to myself crouched on the floor in front of Petersen's desk. I rolled onto my back and stared at the ceiling. I felt bloated and nauseous.

I lost track of how long I lay there but when I next thought of Petersen the afternoon daylight had given way to the gloom of evening.

Petersen was still sprawled in his chair, his eyes open and staring. A grey pallor had now replaced the crimson flush on his face. Even from where I stood I could see that he was not breathing. I snapped on the desk light and instinctively closed his eyelids.

I telephoned the college security department and informed the officer who answered that I had discovered the Head Librarian in his office and that I believed he was dead. The officer told me to wait by the body, not to touch anything and to keep anyone else out of the room. He promised to be with me directly.

I made use of the time before the ambulance and the security people joined me to make sure that Petersen presented a dignified image in death. I straightened his tie and buttoned his shirt. I lifted him from his slumped posture so that he looked like he had expired while working at his desk. I even placed a document in front of him and combed the white mane of his hair. When I had finished he looked peaceful and at rest.

Then I tidied up the office. In his rage Petersen had flung his briefcase into a corner, spilling the contents across the floor. Other folders had been flung on the floor and onto the desk in an ugly pile. I repacked the briefcase and returned the other documents to their proper places. I returned the filing tray to its correct position on the desk.

When the ambulance team arrived they found me sitting calmly in Petersen's guest armchair and Petersen fit to meet them with final dignity. They had brought a doctor along with them and he pronounced Petersen dead with a glance and opined that cause of death had been a heart attack. There would be some sort of investigation, of course, but everything pointed to his initial conclusion.

The paramedics loaded the body onto a gurney, covered it and wheeled what remained of my friend and mentor out of the office and loaded him into the waiting vehicle. I was left alone.

I sat behind Petersen's desk. I was numb with shock at having just witnessed the death of my friend. My own strange experience I concluded was in fact due to the stress of the whole incident on my own nerves. It might have seemed vivid enough but it was all illusion. I pushed it to the back of my mind and considered what I, as both Petersen's friend and an employee of the college should do next.

CHAPTER THREE

The library remained closed for the next two days. I came to work as normal – where else was I going to go? I sat in Petersen's office in the silence of the empty building and tried again to make sense of what had happened. Eventually I had to settle for my original theory. Petersen had suffered a heart attack and I, overcome with panic or fear, had experienced a blackout that was wholly separate from anything that was happening to my friend in his death throes.

Nevertheless, the images that had been presented to me and the sheer physical sensation of my experience continued to haunt me. I returned again and again, in my mind's eye, to the image of the meadow and the elusive reading woman. When I conjured up the sensations that had overwhelmed me they were so vivid that I relived them over and again with their original intensity until I eventually slumped exhausted over Petersen's desk.

Strangely I also felt that the library itself or rather its denizens, the books, had somehow intensified their calling to me. In the few intervals that I managed to put Petersen, his death and all that that had entailed from my mind, I wandered among the shelves as if answering a siren call. The pull on me –that's the only way I can characterise it – became more intense as I left the main floor of the library and descended to the basement area where the older volumes, not so much in demand, were stored. It was as if all that ancient and seldom regarded knowledge was calling me, demanding to be released from the tinder dry and dusty pages.

Late on the afternoon of the second day after Petersen's demise the college Principal put in an appearance. It was then that I found out that Petersen had been suffering from a serious heart condition for some time. His own doctor was in no way surprised and had long expected this outcome. He had been urging his patient to retire. At the library, however, Petersen had very successfully hidden his condition and carried on as if nothing was the matter.

Now that the cause of death had been satisfactorily established and the death certificate issued the Principal wanted the library to be opened again. It was made clear that I was to be in temporary charge while a replacement for Petersen was selected by due process. When he left, the Principal offered no encouragement that I might think myself to be under consideration for the job. He was an image of indifference and coldly business-like.

Before he swept out of the building however, in a few clipped sentences that did not invite discussion, he did inform me of a college decision that could explain what had aroused such a violent and fatal reaction in my colleague Petersen.

The only notable figure that had graced our small town and its college was a minor poet whose small fame had over the several decades since his death been eclipsed by newer and more modern voices. Petersen had known the man briefly and had been an enthusiast for his work. It was Petersen, in fact, who had secured the poet's archive of papers for the college.

On the afternoon of his death Petersen had attended a College Board of Governors' meeting where he had been informed that the archive was being sold to an investment company. He had returned to his office, seething with rage at what he considered a desecration of the trust reposed in him personally. The outcome was sadly inevitable.

Apparently the possibility of the disposal of this college asset had been under discussion for some time and Petersen had been involved in a lone struggle to preserve the posterity of his literary hero. He had not shared this burden with anyone. The pressure on him must have been intense and could only have made the eventual outcome more certain.

Now it was my task to gather the archive together and organise it's hand-over to the new owners. My sense of guilt – both at my inability to help my friend in life and now to posthumously betray his principles – sat heavily on me.

I made the few necessary calls to the other members of the library staff to inform them that we would be returning to normal on the following day. Then I closed up the library and went to call on Petersen's widow.

Naturally I had gone straight to Betty Petersen as soon as my friend's body had been removed from the library premises. Then she had been surrounded by a number of friends and those professionals who are trained to assist the bereaved. A hug and a few words of condolence were all that could be managed.

Now I knew that we would both be alone with our grief and our emotional burdens. I needed to see Betty for comfort as much as I hoped that I could bring her some small consolation.

When I got to the house I was surprised to find Betty alone. I must have given myself away because she was quick to reassure me:

'Sometimes it's best to be alone with your thoughts. It was good to have everyone around to let the first shock sink in but then a body just wants some space and some peace to reflect.'

She led me into the kitchen and bustled about making coffee that neither of us wanted to drink. Betty was putting on a good front but I could feel the waves of sadness flowing from her.

'It wasn't unexpected you know,' she was saying. 'You can't live with someone for nearly fifty years and not know something's wrong. I suppose I must have done my grieving in advance. I haven't been able to cry…strange…'

But then the tears came and the front crumbled. I held her in my arms and let her cry out her sadness. Finally she was finished and dried her eyes.

She sat with me at the breakfast bar, the coffee cups between us. It was too soon to talk about anything so we sat in silence and let the daylight fade.

When I left there was still no need to say anything. There would be time enough after the funeral.

CHAPTER FOUR

The day of the funeral was grey and cheerless.

I had spent the time leading up to the interment getting the poet's archive ready to hand over to the purchaser. Their lawyer had turned up and we'd spent a solid two days going over the inventory. Then the security truck had arrived and Petersen's treasures were shipped off.

Now we all stood around the grave as the casket was lowered into the ground and the priest spoke the words of the burial service. A bare week had gone by and now here we were writing the final chapter of my friend's life. That time had passed in the blink of an eye.

I looked around at the gathering. The Principal was there of course surrounded by a gaggle of the teaching staff. There were a few friends, couples and one or two single women of about the widow's age, one of whom had a supporting arm around Betty Petersen. I knew Tom and his wife had had no children but it was something of a surprise to find that there were no relatives present at all. So the couple had been alone in the world and now Betty was doubly so.

I looked down into the grave trying to send a last thought to my friend. I was trying somehow to make amends for the final act of betrayal I'd been guilty of in relinquishing the archive that had cost him so dear and with so little resistance on my part. I was certain that there was nothing there in that pit. I'd hoped to sense some response but the grave was indeed silent.

As I withdrew my mind from this dark contemplation I became aware of a buzz of noise in my head, as if hearing fragments of conversation from a distance. I looked around and could only see the faces of the funeral party turned towards the grave. Then I noticed the Principal look away and a more intense but incoherent sound came to me from his direction. I was convinced that I was hearing the emotions of the mourners – their thoughts silent within their minds were audible to me.

Unsettled and unnerved I stood back from the group. The noises in my head subsided and I buried my face in my hands. To any onlooker I was a friend overcome with grief. My mind was racing, however, trying desperately to make sense of what was happening to me.

The waves of emotion that swirled towards me became clearer as, despite myself, I focussed on them. I was wishing desperately that it would stop, that I could be left with nothing but silence, but the noise intensified as I felt grief, regret and guilt assail me from around the graveside.

I turned away as the thud of earth on the coffin lid signalled the approaching end of the rites. At the same time the intensity of whatever was emanating from the mourners began to subside. My head began to clear and I staggered away towards the line of parked cars waiting to carry the funeral party back to the college.

Just there, where the roadway met the grass, stood a figure. I couldn't make out his features but I saw he was tall and thin, wrapped in a dark trench-coat with the brim of his hat pulled down over his eyes.

As I approached he turned and made his way among the grave stones towards the far entrance of the site. He'd put some distance between us when he turned and looked directly at me. I felt an intense chill as our eyes seemed to lock. He turned, hunched against the chill wind that had sprung up and was gone.

The college had laid on a memorial reception after the funeral and the mourners gathered in the sports hall at the campus to drink fizzy wine and listen to the Principal make a short speech in praise of the dead man.

Afterwards the group stood around wondering when it would not be too obvious that they had better places to be and took themselves off. The buzzing in my head was still there but less intense and certainly not as painful as at the cemetery. I found that by focussing on individual streams of sound I could control what I was hearing in my head. I began to understand some fragments of what was being thought and felt around me.

A touch on my elbow brought me back to myself. The Principal was at my side. He leaned in to me and spoke confidentially.

'I wanted to thank you for the work you did in handing over the archive. It couldn't have been easy.'

I began to protest in a self-deprecatory way but he brushed this aside.

'I know how difficult it was for Petersen and I know you were in his confidence. He always spoke very highly of you. But you must understand that the College is experiencing very difficult times and the cash on offer can at least secure its future. It's a lucky thing for us that in some cases art and history can be seen to have a monetary value.'

So there it was. I wondered if my friend was in some way placated beyond the grave. Somehow I doubted it.

With another touch on my arm and a murmured 'keep up the good work' the Principal was gone, moving on to another group who stood nursing glasses now nearly empty.

I was tired and the buzzing in my head was dragging me down. It was a physical pain now and a clear prompt to take my leave. I noticed a few of the other mourners making for the door and made up my mind.

Betty was standing on the fringes of the group, the woman friend who had supported her at the interment still at her side. I made my way over to her and offered my farewells. She drew me to one side and thanked me for coming and then with a note of urgency in her voice she asked me to be sure to come to see her very soon.

She had a look in her eyes that spoke to me of a firm resolution but also of a calmness that was enabling her to transcend these hours of grief. I felt sure of what she had in her mind and assured her that I would come to her. Her grip on my wrist tightened as she whispered:

'Come tomorrow…tomorrow. I'll be waiting.'

CHAPTER FIVE

The next evening I left the library early and walked round to the Petersen house. It was only a few hundred yards from the college campus, set in a quiet and tree-lined street. It was a typical small town, middle-class neighbourhood inhabited by the academics from the college. The Petersens had lived there for most of their married life. It was not a grand house but neat and compact, the lawn well-kept and trim, the cladding freshly painted white.

Betty answered my knock promptly. It was almost as if she had been waiting behind the door in anticipation.

We sat drinking tea. Betty occupied an armchair by the window that gave onto a view of the neatly tended garden. I sat at the end of a well stuffed, chintz covered sofa. Her hand strayed to the cover of a black, leather bound volume. She had been looking over a photograph album, reliving precious moments.

The brave front was still in place but I could not ignore the waves of desperate sadness that flowed towards me like an unstoppable tide. I could see that Betty was uneasy and trying to frame a difficult request.

'You know that Tom was very fond of you, don't you?'

I nodded agreement and fiddled uncomfortably with my cup. I set it down on the table and waited on what was going to be said.

'He wanted you to have all this,' and her gesture encompassed the room and the house. 'He saw you as his heir. Especially for his books. He was certain that only you could appreciate them as he did.'

I was about to respond with an embarrassed banality but Betty held up a hand to stop me.

'It's alright. There's no need to say anything. I wanted you to know, that's all. And I want you to know that I think the same. Both of us want you to have the house and what's left behind.'

Again the trite sentiment that her life would continue for many years formed in my mind but I held it back.

'I don't think I want to go on...now that Tom isn't here. Does that shock you? Or seem unreasonable?'

I fidgeted uncomfortably only too aware of where this was all heading. I shook my head.

'I was sure you'd understand.'

'Are you sure? It's soon...I mean early...you may...' I groped unsuccessfully for the right rejoinder.

'I'd been expecting Tom to...to depart for some time. You can't help thinking about what if...'

Again a silence fell between us. I could feel my friend pleading with me wordlessly, reaching out and hoping that I could understand what she was asking of me. It was all too clear but some inhibition prevented me from allowing myself to acknowledge it.

Betty handed me the album, opened at a page.

'That was Tom and I when we first arrived here.'

A young but still hefty Tom Petersen smiled up at me with his arm about a pretty young woman. The house behind was where we now sat. Betty was not showing me her past; she was simply begging me to understand the plea she was unable to put into words.

Then I realised that I really did have the power to relieve my friend's suffering.

Betty Petersen was probably not consciously aware of what she was pleading for but I sensed her longing for the ultimate release. I knew then that she was ready to leave her mortal existence. I could feel her intense craving to be released from her loneliness and torment.

Any further moral or social constraint left me. I knew that I had to help my friend.

Mentally I made myself reach out to her. Somehow I felt my mind begin to edge towards her and I was sure that I felt a wave of relief flow from her as she understood that her request was to be answered.

I felt myself raised up and looking down I could make out my inert shell still seated on the sofa. Likewise I could see Betty sitting calmly opposite me. I felt a force reach out towards me and draw me across the void that separated us. I yielded to it and felt myself drawn in to what I conceived was the threshold of my friend's mind.

I was standing in a towering space that reached out to a greyness above and on all sides. I felt myself about to rush forward and I fought down the urge. I wanted to avoid the turmoil of what had happened with Tom Petersen. I wanted to be in control of myself and what was to happen.

A figure moved towards me and I saw that it was Tom Petersen himself. I tried to speak to him, to hear him say that he understood, that he forgave, but he looked through me and brushed past. I understood then that this was simply a manifestation of Betty Petersen's thoughts and nothing to do with a spectre of her dead husband.

I moved forward and found that my surroundings began to transform. I found myself on a beach with the sea in the distance. Waves crashed on the shore but there was no sound.

Images, insubstantial and ethereal rose around me; the smoke of Betty's past memories. Then there was nothing but an intense light, white and dazzling, enveloping me in its embrace.

I was in the presence of pure energy. An energy made of an accumulated lifetime of experiences, acquired knowledge and lived emotions. The nature of each element was obscure and irrelevant. It was a lifetime transformed into a life giving concentrate of living energy.

Then I lost all vestige of control and began to feed avidly. All veneers of human restraint fell away from me and I became nothing but a beast cramming myself with nourishment. Without compunction I fed on the contents of Betty Petersen's mind.

At some point in my frenzy of feeding I felt a sagging limpness take hold of my surroundings and knew with elation that my friend's wish had been granted and that she was free of all grief and torment.

It was a passing notion and I fell back to feeding until I suddenly felt myself ejected and forced back into the waiting shell of my human body.

I came back to myself in twilight darkness. As my eyes became accustomed to the gloom I could make out the form of Betty Petersen's body still sitting in the armchair by the window. It had been accomplished.

I dragged myself upright. I was sluggish, like a beast that had fed. And wasn't that what I was? I checked the body for vital signs. She was dead alright. A thin smile of release sat on her mouth. I closed her eyes.

It was then that the reality of my own position dawned on me. I couldn't afford to be the one who 'discovered' the body. It would arouse suspicions that I was poorly equipped to answer. There was no time for self-loathing. I had to look to myself.

Quickly I gathered up my tea things and took them to the kitchen. I washed and dried the cup and saucer and put them back in the cupboard with the other crockery. I checked for any other evidence that anyone other than Betty herself had been there and was satisfied that there was nothing.

Back in the lounge I plumped cushions and straightened rugs. I took a handkerchief and wiped the outer cover of the photograph album and placed it on Betty Petersen's lap.

I took a final look at my friend as I left. She looked at peace. I hoped that that was the case and that I had been of some service to her.

Full darkness had now come on and I let myself quietly out of the front door. I huddled in the shadows of the porch, checking for the presence of anyone who might catch a glimpse of me. The street was deserted. I slipped down the path to the sidewalk and hurried away.

Back at my apartment I hurriedly let myself in and locked the door behind me. I sat in the darkness, staring into the void until exhaustion claimed me.

CHAPTER SIX

The next morning I called in sick.

I sat at the kitchen table and drank coffee. I could not face food, the very thought turned my stomach and another form of satiety was now in control.

It was high time that I tried to understand what was happening to me. Way past high time in fact. I forced myself to look back over the last several days and weeks and confront the events that had brought me to this place.

That I had been instrumental in the death of Betty Petersen was undeniable. To hell with hiding behind a cavil and weasel words! Instrumental? I had killed the poor, distressed fellow human being. She had pleaded with me for release. What I had done was for the sake of mercy. But she was dead and I had taken her life. The question remained, though, how had I done it?

That I had somehow entered her mind, of that I was certain. How I had managed to do such a thing was outside my understanding. I searched my recollection of the experience and could only come up with the idea that I had somehow willed it. It had been the force of my will, directed to that object that had allowed me to penetrate her mind.

While there, inside her mind, I had encountered a source of energy or nourishment that my body and spirit craved. At that point I had lost all control, lost any human restraint and begun to feed in a frenzy. There was no way I could control myself or hold back. I had gorged on Betty Petersen's essence until it was exhausted or the strain of such violation had caused her body to expire.

What of Tom Petersen though? It was certified that he had died of heart failure. How could I have been responsible for his death when he was already in the throes of a seizure when I entered his office? Although what had taken place was misted in a fog of confusion what I recalled was too much like the events of the night before to be denied or dismissed. I had entered Tom Petersen's mind. I was there inside him when he expired. I was feeding on his essence when he died. I had weakened him in his struggle for life. Instead of helping him I had pushed him beyond the edge of extinction.

I had to face it. I had the death of two people on my hands. One was seemingly outside of my control but the other was very much due to an act of volition on my part.

I was disgusted. I had become some monstrous parasite feeding off the raw energy of knowledge and experience stored in the minds of my victims. I saw myself as a loathsome worm enjoying vicariously the fruits of other human lives.

But how had I become such a monster? How had I acquired this obscene and deadly appetite? There was no way for me to tell. The questions were irrelevant anyway. I was what I had become.

At least now my affinity with books had an explanation beyond a simple liking for their form and value. The books had been feeding me all my life. They were a repository of that pure energy I found in the human mind and I had supped at them until I found a purer and more satisfying form of that same energy stored in the minds of my victims.

Victims. Two victims of my animal appetite. I resolved then that there would be no more. If I had to remove myself completely from human society, there would be no more. Like a monk I would have to fight down my baser nature.

I forced myself to stand in front of the mirror and take a good long look. Apart from the sag of exhaustion nothing had changed. There was no monster just a plain and unremarkable man. Sandy hair beginning to recede and horn-rimmed glasses. Thin in a geeky sort of way. A sandy moustache sprouted over my top lip. I was still wearing the shirt and dark trousers from the day before. They were crumpled and I looked dishevelled. There was a day old growth of stubble on my face. But that's all there was, just an ordinary joe. A man you would pass in the street without a second look.

Inside though, I knew what lurked. Inside there was a killer. Emotion overcame me and I wept. I wept for the Petersens but most of all I wept for myself.

Later, towards evening, the college Principal came to my door. The look on his face was grave and concerned as he entered my tiny space and took a seat opposite me in the living area.

'I'm sorry to disturb you when you're unwell,' he began uneasily and cleared his throat.

'I thought I should come and tell you in person. These things are too sensitive to be done on the telephone,' and he lapsed into an uneasy silence.

This was a different person to the usually brusque and impersonal head of our institution. The waves of sympathy and distress that flooded from him were palpable. I knew what he had to say – of course I did – and I felt sorry for him.

'It's Betty Petersen,' he began in a rush. 'She was found dead this morning. The maid found her seated in an armchair with a picture album on her knees.'

I turned away and buried my face in my hands to avoid giving myself away. Strangely, although I already knew, hearing the news from another made Betty's death more concrete and a new wave of sadness and guilt welled up inside of me. I felt the Principal's hand on my shoulder.

'I'm sorry for bringing you such awful news...and so soon after Petersen. If it's any consolation they tell me that she looked peaceful and hadn't seemed to experience any distress when she passed. It must have been over quickly.'

The Principal didn't linger and soon made himself scarce, telling me not to hurry back to the library and to take as much time as I needed.

I allowed myself another day, largely for the sake of appearances. I was better off at the library and getting on with work than sitting brooding all alone in the apartment. I had to get on with life and make myself find a way of living with my new and unwonted nature.

In the days that followed it was announced that the authorities had concluded that Betty Petersen had died of natural causes probably due to the shock of losing her husband of so many years. She was buried in a quiet ceremony and laid to rest beside Tom.

As I already knew, I was confirmed as the heir to the Petersen's estate. All of which was an overinflated way of saying that I became possessed of an old European estate car, a charming small house in a leafy off campus area and the few thousand dollars that Petersen had husbanded from his salary over a lifetime. I moved into the house right away and began what I hoped would be a quiet and uneventful life, unremarked and unremarkable.

At the library I tried to keep myself away from the other members of staff who I was now supposed to manage. It didn't concern me that they must have considered me to be aloof and unfriendly, after all I was protecting them. Protecting them from me.

This isolation in many ways proved beneficial to me. The buzzing in my head that I had first experienced at Tom Petersen's funeral persisted and intensified. It was like an obtrusive tinnitus that echoed throughout my skull. I was hearing the thought fragments of those who happened to be close by me.

I also found that I had developed an ability to read and receive emotions and intentions as they flowed from those about me. It was not mind reading as such, it was rather that I was hearing and feeling the peripheral energy from the minds of those about me. On the few occasions that I allowed myself or was forced to be with more than a handful of people this effect became so painful that I was physically ill and had to distance myself.

Over time the few people around me came to view me as cold and unapproachable and kept their distance. I experienced intense feelings of isolation and loneliness. I was viewing humanity as an outsider as if through an impenetrable glass wall. Paradoxically while seeking to separate myself I was often overcome with a craving for human company. I didn't want to engage with others but merely to feel myself as part of a society. When all of this became too much the best I could do was to visit the cafeteria or some other place of anonymous gathering and sip at the feeling of togetherness and human warmth.

I had made my mind up though and had become my own judge and jury. The sentence was for life, a life of isolation. Tom Petersen had been an accident. Betty had been an act of mercy. I did not want to kill again just to satisfy my new and inhuman appetite. There could be no reprieve, the sentence stood.

CHAPTER SEVEN

'You've got yourself a nice place here. Got yourself settled in too.'

I looked up from the papers I was working on. The intruder standing in my doorway looked only too familiar. I couldn't place the face but from his build he was the watching man from the cemetery that day of Petersen's funeral; tall, thin and still wearing the black trench coat. He took off his hat and tossed it onto a chair. His face was gaunt with chisel features, all angles and sharp corners. He was like the blade of a cut throat razor.

'What...'

He came into the room and stood facing me across the desk.

'I said you've made yourself comfortable. Got your feet under the desk. You look the part.'

'Who are you?'

He drew out his badge and flipped it open. He held it out to me and kept it there to be sure I had time enough to read and absorb what was written on the warrant card. Lieutenant Stride, Detective Lieutenant of the city police force. When he was sure I'd registered who he was and the import of his visit he flipped it shut and returned it to his pocket.

I'd been expecting something like this. Dreading a visit from the police. I must have flinched involuntarily because Stride grinned showing a row of wolfish teeth.

'You've been expecting me?'

'No. Not at all,' the response came out too quickly, too pat.

'I think you have. After what you did I'm pretty sure you must have expected someone to notice and to come looking.'

I made myself take a breath; made myself weigh the response. Better, I told myself to be cooperative, make a show of hearing him out and save the denials for later. We locked eyes and time seemed to stand still until I felt compelled to break the silence.

'You're here anyway, so take a seat. Tell me what's on your mind.'

He ignored me and wandered around the office. He looked at the bookshelves, took down a volume and opened it. He leaned against the wall and seemed to be reading. I squirmed in my seat. This seeming indifference was worse than his probing gaze. Without looking up from the page that seemed to be holding his attention Stride suddenly remarked:

'What I'm thinking is that now you've got your boss' job.'

'What?'

'Not only his job but the rest of his life too.'

'I don't believe this...'

'He left it all to you didn't he? You get the house, the car, his savings?'

I tried to control myself, keep things calm. Make a measured response to a ridiculous assertion.

'Look, I've got the job until the college authorities appoint someone. It's temporary. I'm holding the fort.'

'Sure, sure. But you got the house and the rest.'

'I'm not sure that I want to understand what you are getting at here. It's monstrous.'

'You get my drift. But I'll lay it out plain and simple for you. There are two people who are dead. Two people that you were close to. The only people you were close to, in fact. Tom Petersen? You were right there when he died. The wife? I've got a hunch you were close by then as well.'

'You reckon I'd kill my two closest friends...'

'Only friends.'

'You're saying I killed my friends to get hold of this job, an old car, a house and few dollars? What sort of monster do you think I am?'

'There's a question. But murder has been done for less.'

There it was at last. The awful word. Murder. And yes, that was what I was now certain I had done.

At last Stride replaced the book and took a seat. He sat back in the visitor's chair, crossed his legs and eyed me coldly across the desk. There was a silence that I refused to fill.

'I've been looking at you. Checking you out. You don't seem to be a man with much ambition. Not making your way in the world. No lady in your life. Small apartment. No life outside this place. Maybe you woke up one day and wanted something better.'

I started to protest but Stride held up a hand to stop me.

'I checked out the Petersens too. The house, it's nice, spacious. Some of Petersen's books too, antiquarian I'm told, worth something, a tidy something. You like books don't you? Then Petersen had been a saver. We are talking about a good sum in the bank. Must have all looked pretty good to someone in your position. Pretty good motive in my book.'

'Tom Petersen died of a heart attack.'

'And you were standing right by him. Right in this office. That's where it happened, didn't it?

The body laid right there,' and he gestured to the spot where poor Petersen had expired.

'You sure you didn't do anything to help him on his way?'

'There was nothing I could do. I passed out myself. You must remember that detail if you've been looking at this so closely.'

Stride let that hang in the air. Despite myself I felt compelled to add:

'And Betty Petersen? That was natural causes.'

'No unnatural causes were found.'

'And I wasn't there when the maid found her.'

'Ah, but you had been there. The night before. Time of death looked to be sometime the evening before she was found. You had been there.'

'Alright, but Betty was alive and sitting in the chair where she was found when I left the house'

'That was about 10.30 I understand.'

'You understand?'

'You were seen leaving. A dog walker saw you. Said you looked furtive. Why furtive? Were you leaving a house with a corpse in it? A corpse that you put there? And the timing is right around the estimated time of death...'

'Estimated. You have two dead people. Cause of death heart attack and probably a broken heart. People do die from grief you know. And no evidence that there was any foul play.'

'That's what my Captain told me. He told me to drop it. He told me I had plenty of other real crimes to get on with.'

Relief and anger flooded over me. Stride had nothing on me. The police department had no interest in what had happened to the Petersens. Stride was trawling on his own behalf trying to draw me out. I lashed out:

'So you're just here on a fishing expedition. Is that it? You burst in here and start throwing accusations around hoping that I'll break down and confess to some imaginary crime. Don't you realise how much the Petersens meant to me? Don't you realise how much I'm hurting inside?'

Stride uncoiled himself from his seat. We faced each other over the desk.

'You did it alright. You offed Petersen and the old lady. I've got you on motive and I've got you on opportunity. I just haven't figured out your method. But I'll get there. You're smart and you've got all these books to help you. But I'll figure it out, trust me. '

He picked up his hat and left. His words, however, hung in the air.

I reached for the telephone. A call to his Captain of Detectives would get him off my back. I began to dial the number but a thought made me hesitate. What if instead of cooling things a call to Headquarters ramped up attention? What if Stride's visit had actually been sanctioned by his superiors? Better to be cautious. Better to wait and let myself cool down. I hung up the phone.

CHAPTER EIGHT

Stride's visit had unsettled me and for a couple of days I was constantly looking over my shoulder and expecting another visit. I supposed that the policeman would harass me until sheer exhaustion forced a confession from me.

When nothing of the kind happened I began to relax. The man had said that his superiors had told him that there was no case to investigate. He'd probably been reprimanded again for wasting his time and told to leave me alone. He was probably in some other part of town investigating a burglary.

Life carried on and I kept a low profile. Every day, after the library had closed and the place was deserted I wandered among the books. The thin energy that emanated from them provided me with some form of nourishment and kept the pangs of hunger that might make me want to feed more deeply at bay. In the main library it was like sipping a thin and watery gruel. Lower down in the storage shelves the neglected volumes gave off a more satisfying and savoury essence but even then it was a poor diet.

At the weekend I tried to stay away from people, locking myself in my new abode. I had Petersen's books to sustain me and I fed on them. Often though the need to go among humanity overcame me. It was not essential to become involved with any group; simply to be among a throng was relief enough from my isolation.

I began to frequent places where people gathered casually. These places were safe enough as I couldn't risk entering anyone's mind to feed and leaving my own inert body shell on display in a public space. I frequented coffee shops and cafés, the foyer of the city's theatre and even attended performances. I avoided the cinema. The cover of darkness would be too much of a temptation to resist.

One morning I was sitting over a cup of cappuccino in what had become a regular haunt when I found that I had acquired a shadow. The hat was the first thing I noticed. It was placed casually on the table next to a half-empty cup. The hat's owner lowered the newspaper that he had been reading and I saw Stride. He gave me a thin lipped smile with no warmth in it and went back to his paper.

I was shaken. I left my coffee still cooling on the table and left hurriedly.

On another occasion I was doing my weekly shop at the local Walmart, pushing my cart among the shelves. I looked up from the cereal packets and there, along the aisle, leaning on a cart of his own was my shadow. He nodded to me and moved away but he wasn't about to leave me alone. I turned into the next aisle and there he was again, his cold grey eyes seeking me out.

Late on a Sunday morning I chanced to look out onto the street. A black saloon car was parked directly across from my house. I paid it no attention; cars came and went all the time. A little later I looked out and that same car was still there. I looked more closely and saw a figure behind the wheel. Lieutenant Stride.

And so it went on, day to day, week to week. Everywhere I went and everything I did, I expected to see my shadow. But that was the most irksome thing about this whole affair. Sometimes he wasn't there. Sometimes there were whole days, even weeks, where Stride didn't put in an appearance. I'd almost allow myself to relax when up he popped again.

It dawned on me then that this surveillance was not official. This was something Stride was doing on his own and in his spare time. The gaps when I didn't see my tormenter must have been when he was prevented by the call of his duties.

I began to wonder about him. Was he married? Were there children? How had he come to make me the object of an obsession?

Once I understood that Stride was engaged in some crusade of his own and that he had no official backing I started to become amused by his persistent presence. I'd return his smile, give him a cheerful wave. There was nothing to fear, I told myself. In fact Stride's interest strangely seemed to temper the loneliness and isolation of my own position.

I checked myself then. This man was dangerous. I was becoming too complacent. I tightened the restraints on my behaviour.

I told myself that there was nothing to worry about as long as I was careful and never let myself lose control. Control was everything. Stride had no real evidence. He'd give up eventually. All I had to do was be careful.

CHAPTER NINE

It was inevitable that the poor diet afforded me by my friends the books should prove inadequate for my needs. It was then that I knew the hunger.

At first I began to feel run down and always tired and lacking energy. It was like I had a cold coming on. Then my limbs started to feel heavy and the headaches started. My head felt like it was full of mush and I couldn't concentrate. It was like an attack of the 'flu.

I took time off work and lay on my bed drifting in and out of sleep. Then the cramps began. The pain of them griped my insides and I was shivering and burning hot at the same time. I must have passed out because when I came back to awareness my clothes were coldly damp and clung to my skin.

I made myself roll off the bed and tried to stand. My legs refused to support me and I fell to my knees and then lay on my belly. By pure instinct I crawled from the bedroom and found sanctuary and relief in the small office that Tom Petersen had set aside for his books.

I felt their energy and the pains abated sufficiently for me to drag myself into Petersen's old captain's chair. I reached down a volume, an edition of Defoe's 'Robinson Crusoe' and held it to my tortured gut, letting its energies sooth and nourish me.

I knew that this would not hold me for long. I knew that I had to feed. I made myself get to my feet and forced myself into the night.

I was a hunter now as I prowled the darkened streets. I knew well enough where I was going.

On the edge of the town there was an area of parkland. During the day children played ball games, at night other games were on offer.

As soon as I reached the park I saw a figure coming towards me. I looked about me straining all my senses to check that there were no other eyes on me in the darkness. The woman came towards me. She smiled and gave me a 'good evening'.

It didn't matter to me what she wanted or what she was about. I entered her mind and fed voraciously, draining her of her life.

Sated, I allowed myself to fall from her and found myself standing over her crumpled frame. It had been the work of moments.

I dragged the corpse into a stand of trees and scrubby bushes.

Now that the hunger had been assuaged I could think clearly again. The animality dropped away from me and I became a rational being once again. Now that I was safe from the passing observer I took time out to consider my position.

The woman's dead body had no mark upon it. She was dead but from no discernible cause. Stride would immediately conclude that I had been involved and bring an accusation to my door. Contact with Stride in any shape or form was not desired.

The woman was wearing a gaudy scarf. I wound it round her neck and drew the improvised ligature tight. When I released it the bruising was there. Evidence of strangulation. The police would also probably find evidence of sexual activity. So, a sex crime. No mystery there.

I made it back to the house before dawn broke and let myself in. I lay down on the still damp sheets and slept the first real sleep I had enjoyed in days.

I realised then that to avoid being placed in a desperate position I had to feed properly and before the symptoms of the hunger took hold. I had to be careful though and ensure that the inevitable results of my feeding would not come to the attention of Stride and his colleagues. I had been lucky with my victim in the park, a means of covering up my involvement had presented itself and I had had time to take advantage of it. Such a lucky stroke could not be guaranteed in the future.

I had to become a hunter but each hunt would need to be carefully planned.

I sensed that my hunting ground would need to be somewhere outside of the town and far enough for the city police not to become involved. When I took my victim I would need to be unobserved; my own body would be inanimate while I was consuming my victim. Finally I would need to get close enough to my chosen victim to enable me to cross the gap between us and enter their mind. It would also be helpful if the victim was in a state of readiness with their defences down and almost welcoming my penetration.

Over time a plan of campaign crystallized. When the hunger pangs made themselves apparent again I was ready.

As full darkness arrived I climbed into the car and headed out of town. It would have been too obvious simply to head over to the next town. I had reasoned that my hunting ground needed to be a good distance from home. I thought maybe a hundred miles and a different State would be sufficient for my purposes. I checked the rear view mirror from time to time and there was no sign of Stride's car. Maybe he was otherwise employed that night. I sincerely hoped that was the case.

I was also not hunting at random. I had a location and the nature of my quarry in view. My research had been meticulous.

I pulled into the parking lot of the night club, parked beside a shiny truck that had obviously never been used for anything other than cruising and killed the engine. I made sure that I was hidden from the road and waited. A couple of other cars arrived over the fifteen minutes that I waited but Stride's black sedan was not one of them.

I got out of the car and went inside the club. The company inside was mixed, men and women, but divided along gender lines. Groups of men and male couples sat together, women stayed with women although over to one side a mixed group seemed to be having fun. Some single men and women were also in the room, mainly seated or standing in the bar area.

A three-piece band occupied the stage at one end of the room but they kept the volume of their set low enough for a buzz of conversation to dominate.

I took a seat at the bar and ordered a soda. I turned to face the band. I had nearly finished my drink before a man stood beside me. He was casually dressed, blue jeans and plaid shirt. He was tall, maybe approaching middle age and wearing glasses.

'Can I get you another?'

I agreed, we shook hands and exchanged names. Teddy took a seat beside me and we talked irrelevance. A second round of drinks came and was drunk. Teddy suggested a breath of fresh air and a quieter place to get acquainted. It seemed just too easy.

Outside I scanned the parking lot looking for signs of Stride. Nothing. Teddy noticed and took my precautions for nervousness. He took my hand and gave it a squeeze.

'It'll be nice, don't you worry.'

He led me to the truck that was parked next to my Volvo. How convenient. We climbed in and onto the bench seat. His hand was on my leg. I let him lead the situation. When he put his arms around me and offered his mouth I entered his mind with ease. Inside I fed on his essence until I felt his death shudder. I continued to feed and when he was empty I eased myself from him and back into my own body.

I felt nothing, no emotion, no regret or disgust. I was doing what I had to do. If anything I was quietly pleased that I seemed to controlling the whole process much better. It had become an enjoyment to savour as well as a means of sustenance.

I shimmied out of the cab, leaving the husk of Teddy slumped over the seat. He looked drunk and the casual observer would probably conclude that he was simply sleeping it off.

I got into the Volvo and fired up the engine. A couple of hours later I was pulling into my drive and was pleased to see that friend Stride was nowhere in sight. I climbed into bed and slept the sleep of the innocent.

For the next few days I scanned the newspapers but there was no mention of the demise of Teddy. He'd been just a middle-aged man who had passed away on a night out. Likewise Stride put in a couple of his routine appearances but he never approached me. It seemed that I had achieved my objective of a quiet life.

CHAPTER TEN

The autumn semester had started and new faces began to appear as the freshman intake found their way to the library. Among those new faces was Patsy-Anne Colby.

I first became aware of Patsy-Anne when I was filling in behind the issuing counter during the lunch-time session.

With a friendly smile she pushed her books across the counter towards me. I checked her student card noting her name and stamped the return dates in them. I noted her selections; a D H Lawrence and Stephenson's 'Kidnapped'. I pushed the two volumes back to her and handed her back her card.

'English Literature major? I didn't think these were on the required reading list...'

'No, math. But I love to read. These are for relaxation.'

She was a pretty girl in an understated way. Tending to plumpness but not too much so. Above all she had a nice smile. It really did light up her face. I watched her as she walked away and left through the swing doors.

Next day I went to the refectory for lunch, feeling the need to be with people. I took my usual seat at the back of the dining hall so that I was with the throng of diners but not part of them. I blotted the buzz of emotions and thoughts from my consciousness and concentrated on my food.

'Hi there. Mind if I join you?'

Patsy-Anne had managed to come right up to my table without me noticing her approach. Without waiting for a response she put down her tray on the table opposite me and drew up a chair.

'Remember me?'

I nodded, 'Lawrence and Stephenson. How could I forget?"

'Is that how you think of all your friends? By the books they read?' Her smile was playful, cajoling. She might have been flirting with me.

I mumbled a response and bent over my food. I was at a loss how to behave in this situation. I didn't really like eating with anyone let alone a perfect stranger.

'Have you read 'Treasure Island'?' I found myself asking.

'Have I? My dad gave me a copy for my fourteenth birthday. I wanted to be Jim Hawkins but I'm a girl.'

She was certainly a girl. An attractive girl. This sort of thing didn't happen to me and I found I was liking it.

We talked books for a while. I asked about her course and her room at the College. She was enjoying the course and her room was just fine. I let her finish her food and then excused myself, claiming a need to relieve a colleague back at the issuing desk.

The weekend rolled around and on Saturday morning I went to my usual haunt for coffee. I'd been sitting over my tall latte for about five minutes when Patsy-Anne came through the door and made a bee-line for me. She didn't ask this time, just sat alongside me and slid a bag of books under the table.

'So this is where you hang-out on the weekend.' She breezed.

The waitress came and she ordered a latte, just like mine. She invited me to share a pastry. I declined but she went right ahead and ordered. When it came she used a fork to divide it and pushed a half towards me.

She talked. I listened.

Stridc was in his usual corner. I could see that he was curious by the especially intense scrutiny he gave us. It was after all a strange sight; me with a woman. Me in company with anyone was a strange sight.

The middle of the following week I was at my desk working on a report for the Governing

Board when one of the assistant librarians announced that a young woman was asking for me at the issuing desk. For some reason I was not surprised that the person in question was none other than Patsy-Anne. Strangely it felt good to see her and to think that she had sought me out.

I forget what she wanted to see me about. It was obviously a pretext and the matter was trivial. I think she might have coffee stained a book and wanted to confess.

After Patsy-Anne had left the library the assistant who had announced her remarked:

'That girl's got a thing for you. Lucky fellow…'

I gave him a withering look that only served to enhance my reputation as a miserable misanthrope. Still, despite my resolve to isolate myself from society I felt warm inside at the attention I was getting.

Patsy-Anne continued to show up and on those occasions when she didn't appear I found that I was missing her. It was as if we had become a couple without noticing. It certainly seemed we had a lot in common. I even secretly let myself hope that she might be like me. That she might share my own appetites.

The way of life I had sentenced myself to was becoming hard to bear. Isolation was tough even though I had known that I was an outsider for most of my life. Being unique was quite another load to bear. And so queerly unique at that. I craved companionship. A true companionship where you can share hopes and dreams and the trivia of life. Above all I needed someone to talk to and to share my innermost and darkest feelings.

I knew deep down that it was an illusion. Patsy-Anne was just a normal and maybe needy girl, adrift from her family for the first time and needing a friend, an affectionate friend. She couldn't know what a poor choice she was making.

That Patsy-Anne was pursuing me with intent became only too clear when she asked me out to dinner. There was no avoiding it, what was on offer was a date and all that that might entail.

I was not a complete innocent. There had been girl-friends. Seldom and far apart but still I had enjoyed female company in the past. Quite a distant past to be truthful and I had never really become accomplished with the behaviours expected on a date.

Patsy-Anne had caught me at point in time where I was feeling hopeful that the illusion could be made real so I accepted her proposition without thinking through the consequences. I knew immediately that I made a bad if not fatal move.

The date was not exactly a disaster but I'm sure that the outcome was not as Patsy-Anne had anticipated.

We went to a little Italian bistro close by the college campus. The meal was great and the wine tasted rich and fruity. We talked easily now, mainly about books, we were relaxed in each other's company. My heart even rose momentarily when Patsy-Anne started to talk about the effect that libraries had on her. Her experiences exactly matched my own. I told myself that she must have felt the same energies in the presence of books that I did.

When we left the restaurant I was filled with hope. Maybe I hadn't made a disastrous move after all. Maybe some mysterious force – karma, fate, whatever- had provided the companion that I needed.

We went to retrieve the Volvo and in the darkness of the parking lot Patsy-Anne took the next and obvious step. She took me in her arms and kissed me. It was a delightful sensation and I kissed her back.

I felt myself slipping and tumbling. I was entering Patsy-Anne's mind despite myself. I was inside her and felt the life essence in her mind. I fought the desire to feed, to consume her energies. I made a supreme effort of will and dragged myself away from her and slipped back into my own body.

That effort had cost me dear. I doubled over as pain seared my gut and blackness clouded my sight. I felt Patsy-Anne's shock and concern. I felt her hands on me as she tried to steady me and prevent me sprawling at her feet.

Somehow she got me upright and helped me to the car. I sat in the passenger seat with sweat pouring over my face. My breath was coming in deep, ragged draughts as I fought to stay conscious. I heard the engine start.

I must have blacked out completely because when I came to we were in the driveway of my house. Patsy-Anne was behind the wheel. I fumbled for the door release and tumbled out of the car. I supported myself leaning against the car as rubbery legs threatened to dump me on the concrete. Patsy-Anne came around, got an arm round me and eased me to the door.

I mumbled something about eating shellfish as she felt in my jacket pocket for the latch key and opened the door.

I pulled myself from her and stumbled across the threshold. I positioned myself to bar her entry. She seemed to get my message.

'Are you going to be alright?'

'Shellfish...shouldn't eat shellfish. Be alright when I get to bed. Sleep it off. Sorry...sorry.'

I pushed the door shut in her face. I waited in the dark until I heard her slam the car door shut and saw the car key poked through the letterbox and clink onto the doormat. I steadied myself and climbed the stairs. Out of the bedroom window I saw Patsy-Anne disappear round the corner of the street and into the night.

I spent the next few days laying low in an attempt to avoid Patsy-Anne. The telephone in the house rang a couple of times each evening but I ignored it. I didn't bother to check for messages.

It was late that night. I had stayed on at the empty library pretending to work but really using the fact that no-one could get in once the staff had left for the day to ensure that I couldn't be ambushed by Patsy-Anne. When I thought that it was safe enough to venture outside I walked home.

As I came up my driveway I saw a figure huddled in the porch. Patsy-Anne – of course it was her -got to her feet and came towards me. Her tone was almost pleading:

'Are you alright? I've been so worried about you. You aren't answering your phone.'

'You saw I was ill…'

'That's why I was worried. I've been waiting here for hours. Where have you been?'

'I've had to catch up on work.' I lied. 'I had to take time off. You shouldn't have just turned up like this.'

I meant it and I hoped that Patsy-Anne would read my intention clearly. No such luck.

'I'm chilled to the bone. Won't you ask me in?' Now she really was pleading. The need in her voice was explicit.

I couldn't let her in. If I did I knew only too well where she would try to take things. I needed to get a locked door between her and me. But then I didn't want to invite a scene of tears, recrimination and raised voices on my doorstep.

'Look – it's really great of you to come round. I really appreciate it. I feel awful that you sat out here. But I'm not over it yet. I shouldn't have gone to work. Look. I think I might be infectious. I've got a rash coming out. I don't want to make you ill. You do understand, don't you?'

She seemed to swallow it. Maybe it was better than an outright rejection. She took a few steps back as if she really believed that I was carrying some disease.

'Look, I'll make it up to you...when I get over all this. I'll call you. Maybe you could come over then.'

She nodded agreement and after more enquiries about my welfare she turned away and made her way into the night. I slipped inside the house and bolted the door.

I knew then that all this had to end. I couldn't have this girl turning up everywhere I went. What's more her pursuit was becoming even more dogged than my arch nemesis Lieutenant Stride.

It was absurd. I hadn't pursued her, hadn't sought her company but here I was trying to break up with her. Worse, I didn't have the faintest idea how to do it.

After some thought I invited myself back to Patsy-Anne's room. Better, I thought, to be inside somewhere when I broke the news. There would be a scene for sure and I didn't want attention drawn to us. Patsy-Anne seemed delighted. She was obviously expecting a different outcome. When I arrived she threw herself at me, wrapped her arms around me and planted a kiss square on my mouth.

I pulled loose from the entanglement of her arms and pushed her away. She began to protest; still not understanding that I was not entering into what she thought was the spirit of the evening.

'Listen to me Patsy-Anne,' I started. 'I'm flattered that you want to spend time with me. I'm not right for you. I know this...this. This isn't going to work out. I want to stop right now.'

No words came from her. She stood there in front of me not moving, her mouth agape.

'Do you understand? I want you to leave me alone. Don't come round to my house. Don't ask for me at the library. Just leave me alone.'

Her face crumpled and tears cascaded down her cheeks. She touched me then. I felt a pang of affection and took her in my arms and held her to me. I didn't want her to hurt, to feel sorrow. I felt her mind reaching out to me and I tried to fight down the desire to respond. She fought me then, dragging me into her. I yielded and lost all control. Inside her mind I began to feed voraciously. I felt the death tremor shudder through her frame. I felt the force that ejected me from her and found myself standing over the inert body of Patsy-Anne who had been so alive but a few minutes before.

I had to think quickly. I had only been in the room for a few minutes. The body that was crumpled on the carpet was fully clothed. I knew that there were no apparent injuries. Leave well enough alone.

The main danger would be if anyone had heard us or was about and able to see me make my exit. It was a student house, after all. There were bound to be eyes and ears about.

I eased open the door and peered around the edge. No-one. I risked slipping into the corridor and looked around. Still no-one. I pulled the door shut and heard the deadlock click into place. I turned to leave and saw her.

A girl student in sports kit had come out into the corridor just as I was backing away from the door. Had she seen me coming out of the room? She came towards me.

'Can I help you? Oh, you're the head librarian. Are you looking for someone?'

It looked like she hadn't seen me leaving Patsy-Anne's room. My mouth was dry as I gestured to the door:

'I was hoping to see Patsy-Anne. It doesn't seem like she's in though.'

I tapped on the door. The girl and I waited in silence.

'Well, doesn't look like I've caught her in. I'll catch up with her later. Never mind.'

'I could give her a message. If that would help?'

‘Just tell her I was looking for her. It’s about a book she requested.’

‘That’s service,’ the girl joked with smile. ‘She must have something.’

‘Thanks – it was just that she said she needed it urgently and I was around anyway.’

‘Ah, Okay. I’ll tell her.’

‘Thanks’

I accompanied the helpful girl out of the building and she set off at a trot for the sports hall, leaving me alone in the gathering night.

CHAPTER ELEVEN

As usual I was the last to leave the library that night. After I had secured the main door I scanned the night's darkness for any sign of Lieutenant Stride. There was no-one waiting in the blackness for me. Relieved I walked quickly, covering the short distance to my front door and the safety of the house.

I locked the entrance door behind me and allowed myself to breathe easier. As I entered the living room the flame of a lighter pierced the darkness. An unseen hand guided it to the tip of a cigarette. The flame disappeared leaving only the orange glow of a pinpoint of burning tobacco.

I flicked on the light to reveal detective Stride sitting back in the armchair by the window. He drew deeply on the cigarette and blew a cloud of smoke.

'How..?'

'Did I get in here?' he supplied. 'I'm a cop. I hang out with bad people; sometimes stuff rubs off. You been expecting me?'

'No. What do you want?' I lied.

Stride dragged on the cigarette for a last time and stubbed it out. He shook his head in a mocking admonition.

'You've really done it this time. And I thought you were so careful. Can't you think why I'm here? Go on, try really hard.'

There was a silence as he eyed me coldly.

'We found your girl-friend.'

'I don't have a girl-friend.'

'No more you do friend. When we found her she was stone cold.'

'Stop playing games. Speak plainly.'

'I guess we have to do this the hard way. You know a woman by the name of Patsy-Anne, Patsy-Anne Colby?'

'Yes, I do.'

'Sure you do. You've been seen with her. Often. You looked to be close. I'd have said she was a girl-friend.'

'She wasn't.'

'If you say so. It hardly matters what she was to you. She was found dead, couple of days ago. Not a mark on her.'

'And you are implying that I had something to do with her death?'

'I'm not implying anything pally. I'm telling you. This has your hallmark all over it. Corpses without a mark, no obvious explanation of why they died but dead all the same. You're knee deep in them.'

'I was nowhere near her...'

'When she was killed? I think you were. We put the time of death around 8.00pm Monday evening. She was found Wednesday morning when she hadn't shown up for classes.'

'I wasn't anywhere near her...'

'You were seen.'

The girl in the sports kit! It must have been her.

'And she'll tell you I was knocking on Patsy-Anne's door and getting no answer.'

'That was your story. Some malarkey about a book she needed. The girl didn't believe you. Neither do I.'

'Alright. I'll come clean. I'll tell you what really happened.'

'I recommend it – truth always comes out in the end. So what's the story? I'm sure it's going to be good.'

'I did know Patsy-Anne.'

'That's a given – you've been seen around with her enough.'

'Truth is she threw herself at me. I was flattered and went along with it for a while. Then she started to get more intense. I wasn't interested and that night I told her so.'

'And?'

'That's it. She started to cry and I left.'

‘So what was all that about with the girl in the hall outside. Why the story and the pantomime with knocking on the door? And by the way, why didn’t Patsy-Anne open the door?’

‘I was embarrassed. The scene with Patsy-Anne had unnerved me. I wasn’t thinking straight. It’s not something I do every day.’

‘I think that Patsy-Anne was already dead and lying on the floor. There was no way she was going to answer the door. And you knew it. I don’t like your story mister. Want to hear mine?’

‘I have a choice?’

‘Smart mouth doesn’t suit you. Here’s the thing. You went there expecting to get your jollies. Patsy-Anne wouldn’t play. You got mad, she got dead. I don’t know how you did it, but you did kill her.’

‘You’ve got me outside her door and a pretty theory all your own. What does your boss make of it?’

‘Same as before. Looks like natural causes so drop it. He wants it to go away.’

‘And you?’

‘I know I don’t have a case. I’ve been doing this for a few too many years not to know that.’

‘So you’ll be leaving me alone?’

‘Not that easy. You’ve piqued my interest. I know you offed the Petersen’s and the girl. I know that there are a few other bodies that have popped up too. Nothing that leads back to you – but there's a certain smell.'

'Can't you just leave me alone? I'm tired of this...this harassment.'

'Here's the news. I've changed my mind about you. I thought you were all about gain but it's not that. Why you do it. You enjoy it don't you? I've got my own small town serial killer in you.'

Stride uncoiled himself from the chair and picked his hat from beside the ashtray. At the door he looked back over his shoulder.

'I'll be seeing you around. Count on it'

The front door slammed shut and I stood there trembling. There was nothing that would make Stride drop me. He was going to dog my footsteps until I made the one fatal error he needed to bring me down. It was just a matter of time and persistence. Stride was a man of persistence.

CHAPTER TWELVE

There was only one solution. I had to run and keep on running until I had put enough distance between me and Stride. I had no inkling of what would be enough and right then I was ready to run for the rest of my life.

I held myself in check though. Planning was needed. If I was to disappear without trace I needed to get myself a head start and not arouse suspicion too early. Arrangements needed to be made.

I drew down the money I had inherited from Tom Petersen from the bank and closed the account. I was pretty sure that the few thousand dollars in hard cash would last me until I could find my place of safety. I knew that the form of my place of safety would take a while to define. I just hoped it would be sorted out on the road.

I couldn't just disappear from the college. That would ring alarm bells. I was becoming surprised by how much anchored me to the town. I'd have to resign, work out my notice. Then there was the house and the various supply companies that serviced my life.

I thought that I'd take care of everything after I'd resigned from my job. I prepared an official letter and carried it to the Principal. I wanted to deliver it in person. I didn't want the letter to be tangled in the internal post. His response amazed me.

The Principal glanced at the letter and looked at me over his spectacles.

'Thank you. You've saved me a problem.'

He must have seen the puzzled look that passed across my face.

'I've been wondering how to cut you loose. You've become a real problem. I've had complaints about you from the rest of the library staff. They say you are generally unpleasant and unhelpful. You stay locked in your office. You are unapproachable and remote. I believe that I'm on the point of losing several valued members of staff. I was going to let you go and now you're on your way anyway.'

'Should I...'

'Turn over your keys and your security badge right now if you want. No. On reflection, just hand them over. You can leave now. I'll get the HR department to send on your salary and other stuff.'

He stood and, automatically, offered me his hand. He dropped it to his side a second later when he realised that it was inappropriate. I turned and left.

The telephone company and the utility companies were an easier and less stressful proposition. It took just a telephone call or three and I was clear.

I thought about the property taxes and concluded that I could just forget about them. By the time the Sate and the County got around to realising that I was no longer a resident I'd probably be an old man.

I loaded Tom Petersen's books into the back of the Volvo. It was like Count Dracula loading his coffins with his native earth. I knew I'd need their sustenance on the road and there was a bond there too. They were a part of Tom Petersen.

When I thought that I had effectively cut all ties with my community I got behind the wheel of the Volvo and headed west.

I really did think that I could drive away from it all. That I could simply put a few hundred miles between me and Stride. It was a case of hope over a lack of experience.

I drove on I-90 West skirting the lake shore, just taking short rests at truck stops and holed up in a cheap motel off the Interstate just over the state line in Ohio. I ordered in pizza and drank soda from the vending machine in the motel reception. I showered and stretched out on the bed, easing the kinks in my spine.

It was time to decide. Time to figure out what I was really running towards and where I might find it.

I couldn't leave the USA. No passport. Anyway crossing at the borders would leave a trail a mile wide. So Canada was out. Mexico too, though to be honest that option had little appeal. Overall I guessed it would be easier to hide among my fellow Americans.

Then where to hide? The wild and empty country of Montana or Nevada? I was not made for the wilderness though for sure in some of the empty states a man could disappear for years, for a lifetime. No shack in the woods or clinging to a mountainside for me. The fact was, though, I needed humanity around me. I was a hunter and my prey was, sadly, human.

Small towns, they were my habitat. Small towns where a stranger would draw attention and neighbourly curiosity. Small towns where my night time activities would be easily remarked. I didn't want to bring another local lawman around my neck. Small towns were out.

So it looked like my only option was to hide out in some major city. I might at least find some employment there and hiding in a forest of concrete and humanity did seem the best solution.

If I continued to travel west I'd eventually reach Seattle. San Francisco or Los Angeles also looked promising.

In the end I flipped a coin. Heads Seattle, tails the City of the Angels. It came down tails.

Early the next morning I headed south west with over two thousand miles in front of me. I avoided major towns along the way, slept in the car, tucked away out of sight in woodland or wherever I could find cover from prying eyes. I found food in convenience stores or grabbed coffee and fried meals in roadside diners along the way.

Petersen's books sustained my other appetite, their energy trickling from the back of the car. Apart from that I suppose fear must have kept the hunger at bay until I met poor Abby. Then all control slipped from me and I had fed voraciously. Poor Abby.

So there I was heading south and east through Texas and into Louisiana. Along the way I hunted, selecting my victims from among those who would not be missed. I may not have become wise but I was developing a certain feral cunning. No one would think anything of a homeless man expiring by the roadside or an old woman dying in a trailer, friendless and without family. I came to know the underside of a lot of communities.

I still couldn't accept the idea; that someone had to die so that I could live. It seemed anyway that I didn't have a choice. Feeding was agony to my conscience, the hunger agony for my body.

I thought about ending it all. I'll admit that. I came near one night of dark despair. Maybe I was a coward. Maybe I had a lust for life. Maybe I was impelled to survive at all costs by my newly revealed nature. I know that some people will cling to life no matter what the pain and hardship they have to endure. Maybe I am such an animal.

I was not in a hurry now. I had convinced myself that Abby would prove a brick wall to Stride's enquiries. As long as I was careful and kept out of sight, I could roam freely. I somehow hoped that Stride would forget all about me when fresh leads dried up. Meanwhile Petersen's money was lasting.

I drove on through the southern states. Along the way I changed the Volvo for a second-hand Ford sedan. It was my last link to New England. At the time it seemed a smart move.

A few miles past the state line that divided Alabama from Georgia I rolled into a small town. The main street was clean and inviting. I noted a hotel, the Colonial House. It seemed fresh and inviting with its white painted wooden cladding and dark shingle roof.

I parked up and decided to take a look around. I was tired of driving. I thought maybe I might find somewhere for lunch and rest a while. I'd move on that afternoon.

The sidewalks were busy with normal folk going about their normal business. I saw a book store and walked through the door. The owner smiled a greeting and went back to her knitting. I browsed the shelves drinking in the fresh energy that spilled from the assembled volumes. I picked up a thriller by a well-known author. The cover said it was the thirtieth adventure for his action hero creation.

The owner put down her knitting and bagged my purchase.

'That's a good one. Good choice.'

'I hope so. He's very popular – rightly so. Thank you.'

It felt good to touch another human being. The woman had been friendly. She had a nice smile.

I found a restaurant along the street. It was early and I was alone in the dining room. I ordered and leafed through my purchase. Other diners began to arrive and the familiar tinnitus of their thought and emotion fragments started up in my head. On the road I was isolated from this irritation. I tried, unsuccessfully, to ignore the intrusion.

Outside the restaurant I found that I was beginning to like this little town. It was ordinary. The sun was shining and the air felt clean. My meal must have been too good. I began to feel sleepy. The road had lost its appeal for a while. It would be good to stay in one place for a couple of days. It would be good to shower and sleep in a comfortable bed between crisp, clean sheets.

I checked in to the Colonial House. The lobby smelt of fresh polish and lavender. When the receptionist asked for payment on account I didn't think but pulled out a credit card. It was the action of a moment and I didn't give it a thought.

Upstairs, the room was fresh and airy. I lay on the bed and drifted off to sleep. When I awoke the daylight had almost gone. I undressed and showered and climbed between the sheets. They were crisp and clean, as promised.

The next morning I found my breakfast in a café along the street and set out to explore. Along the street, just past the police headquarters, I found the public library. I went inside. The books reached out to me. There was that delightful odour of dust, paper and floor wax.

I spent the next two hours browsing the shelves, reading the journals and newspapers and sucking in the nourishing energy that spilled from the shelves. Over the next three days I visited the library every day and spent hours in the company of the books and the librarian.

On the third day the librarian, a suet dumpling of a woman who wore wire-rimmed glasses, waddled over to me.

'You seem to like our little library. You always seem to be here.'

Her tone was pleasant with a hint of enquiry. She was opening a conversation with a readily available gambit.

I was glad to chat with her and told her what I was doing in town and what my plans were. It wasn't the truth, of course, but a satisfactory and satisfying story. I gave her a counterfeit version of myself in exchange for her genuine interest.

We soon got around to the subject of books and I let slip that I too was a librarian, but on sabbatical. Her face lit up, which I took for pleasure at meeting a fellow professional.

'What a pity you aren't planning to stay on in town...' she began.

'I'm not in a rush to move on. My time's my own. What do you have in mind?'

I was expecting a dinner invitation or something about a book reading that was scheduled at the library. My new friend seemed a trifle embarrassed but now she had made her opening I could see she felt obliged to continue.

'It's just that...I hope you won't think I'm talking out of turn...well...'

I encouraged her and she finally got to the point.

'I know of someone who's looking to hire a librarian.'

'Do you mean here...with you?'

Nice as that would have been, taking up employment with the State or County authority would not be a wise move. It would be like sending Stride an open invitation to come by for a visit.

'No, no. There's hardly enough for me to do here. But to tell you the truth I quite like it that way. I can go home to Homer at five o'clock every night and not have to worry about the library until the morning.'

I was intrigued. It might be nice to spend some time in one place. I was getting to think that pretty soon I'd be completing a circuit and ending up where I'd started. After Florida there were just the Keys and the Ocean.

'It's a friend of mine...' she was continuing. 'Not really a friend...an acquaintance...Greta.'

'And Greta is?'

'You must have heard of her. She's Greta Franklin. She's in films, the movies. Or she was.'

The information dam was breached and the rest of the story poured out in a torrent. Greta had married into the local aristocracy, giving up her film career. Now widowed she lived alone in the Plantation House surrounded by the collections built up by the family, including a vast library of volumes that dated back to before the War of Independence. She needed someone – a librarian – to catalogue the collection. I supposed her final intention would be to sell them off.

None of that mattered to me. I was intrigued and interested. A collection of books, antiquarian books. That sounded like manna to me. And if this Greta were the only occupant of the Plantation House then so much the better. Here was my solution being handed to me on a plate. A secure and private place, fulfilling employment and payment without the need for any formalities. It was a gift.

I told the dumpling lady that I'd be delighted to take on the task if she would only make the introduction. She bustled off at once to make the call and that afternoon I presented myself at The Planation House.

CHAPTER THIRTEEN

The highway, a two lane blacktop, ran past the location of the Plantation House at about two miles distance. A single lane metalled road ran from the highway up to the rise on which the house was perched. I parked on the open area in front of the house a respectful distance from the entrance porch.

The house was a relic of the antebellum period. It was a stately building over three floors and graced with a classical canopy and columns over the front entrance. A flight of steps led up to the door. I could visualise carriages arriving and footmen in livery in attendance.

An African-American woman, tall and slender, opened to me and listened as I stated my business. She didn't volunteer a word but slightly inclined her head in acknowledgement and motioned me inside.

I followed her through the cool interior, through a grand entrance hall and along a corridor floored in polished wood. She opened a door and allowed me to pass into the room. I heard the door whisper shut behind me.

A fey, insubstantial woman dressed in flowing white half-rose to acknowledge my presence. She subsided back onto the sofa on which she had been seated as if even that simple act had drained her last resources of energy.

'You're the librarian?' her voice barely above a whisper.

I agreed that I was the librarian and that I understood that she might have employment for me. She beckoned me closer and indicated a place for me to sit opposite her.

Now that I was in her presence I knew who she was or rather had been. Although I did not frequent the cinema I had not been living in a cave. She had once been Greta Berry and had featured often in the newspapers and at award ceremonies. I recalled that she had married old money in the form of the only remaining son of a Georgia family. It had caused plenty of scandal at the time as the son was nearly twice her age.

I was shocked to see her in this condition, weary and drained of vitality. She could only be around forty years of age now.

In a barely audible voice Greta explained the task she had in mind. It appeared that her deceased husband's family had amassed a large collection of books over the years, centuries even. Many must be of value but there was no order in the collection. She wanted someone knowledgeable who could catalogue the collection.

I asked if her ultimate intention was to sell the books. She ignored the question.

She continued to explain the terms of my employment. I was to live in the Plantation House. I would be fed and receive a salary. My evenings would be free. Would all that be satisfactory?

I agreed that I should be glad to take on the task. Greta seemed pleased and sank back onto her sofa with an air of extreme exhaustion. She had a small hand bell beside her. She used it and a faint tinkle resulted.

Claudine must have been standing right outside the door to have picked up on such a subdued summons. Had she been listening at the door? She slipped into the room. Greta murmured,

'Claudine will see to you now. She takes care of everything in the house. She'll show you the library and your accommodations. Whatever you need, ask Claudine. Now you must excuse me. I need to rest.'

I followed Claudine out of the room. She led me along corridors and up a flight of stairs to the next floor. There was no attempt to engage in conversation. We didn't exchange one word until she opened a door, stood back and allowed me to pass inside.

The room was bright and airy and smelt of fresh paint. The windows gave a view of the rolling landscape that surrounded the Plantation House. It was comfortably furnished.

'This is your sitting room,' Claudine said finally. 'When you are not working in the library you will confine yourself to your apartment and not go wandering around the house.'

I made some remark about being quite comfortable which was ignored. Claudine brushed past me and opened a second door. She gestured to the interior of this second room.

'This is your bedroom. Any of your things you keep in here.'

She closed the door before I could get a good look inside and she stood looking at me with a cold and considering glare.

In my turn I got a chance to study Claudine closely. She was a good looking woman, in her late thirties or thereabouts. Her skin was a light coffee and cream. She held herself proudly. You just knew you didn't even want to try and mess with her. She was slender but certainly not skinny. There was sweet meat on the bones.

Claudine brushed past me and led me back into the corridor. A few steps along there was another door. Claudine opened it and gestured me inside.

The whole room, which must have been four times as big as the apartment I had just been shown was piled high with books. I could see that there was ample shelving along the walls and in cabinets that were set across the room but most of the volumes were simply stacked on the floor. I looked an enquiry at Claudine who stood in the doorway.

'There was another fellah. Didn't last but a few days. I guess he didn't like the atmosphere here or something. I don't think he really knew what he was about. That's what he did. Just piled them up to make it look like he was working at things. I just hope you are the real deal.'

The books reached out to me. I wandered about picking up a volume at random. What I was looking at was a prime collection. I felt drawn to one stack that teetered dangerously on the corner of some shelving. At the bottom there was a very thick book bound in antique leather, blackened by age.

The book was giving off pulses of pure energy, the like of which I had never experienced in a library bcforc. Quickly I pullcd the other volumes off of it. I staggered back in amazement. I was looking at a Gutenberg bible – probably one of only five or six outside the confines of a museum. This alone was a treasure beyond price.

I couldn't believe my luck. I was giddy with the excitement of being confronted with such riches. I would have delved deeper into this treasure trove but Claudine called me back to myself.

'You'll eat with me in the kitchen. Three meals a day. Be on time and don't keep me waiting. Apart from that you stay out of my way. Looks like you'll have plenty to do.'

I nodded agreement.

'You do not bother Miss Greta. Understand? Anything you want – for your employment – you come to me. Any questions – you come to me. If you need to tell Miss Greta anything – you do it through me.'

I didn't stop to think about what I was saying. The question popped out,

'What's wrong with Miss Greta? How sick is she?'

'I don't care to be questioned about Miss Greta but to stop you wondering I'll give you an answer. No-one knows. Despite what the newspapers said about her and Mister Robert, she married him out of love. When he passed she simply collapsed in on herself. We've had doctors. The best. But they can't suggest anything but grief. The poor woman is simply wasting away. So now you know. And I'll thank you to stay away from Miss Greta and ask no more of your bothersome questions. Do your work and you'll get paid.'

I opened my mouth but Claudine cut me short.

'Greta is mine, mister. You stay away,' she spat at me.

'Greta is mine.' I put it down at the time to a slip of the tongue. She had probably meant to say that Greta was her responsibility. Later I wasn't so sure. Her tone had been distinctly possessive.

It seemed, on that sour note, that our interview was over. Claudine led me back down the stairs and to the entrance hall. It seemed we were not destined to enjoy friendly relations. It mattered little to me at the time. I had found a place to be out of sight and there was the enticement of the books.

I climbed back in the car and drove back into town. I parked up by the Colonial House and walked over to the library to share my good news with my friend.

On the way back to the hotel I noticed a few familiar faces. One or two who passed by me nodded in a friendly greeting. The town was getting under my skin. I liked it here. It felt like home.

The next morning I paid my bill and checked out.

CHAPTER FOURTEEN

Every paradise harbours a serpent.

Claudine made it quite clear from the start that I was to be allowed to stay on at the Plantation House on sufferance. She barely spoke to me. On most days she didn't even muster a 'Good morning.' I was allowed to eat in the kitchen but she never joined me for meals. Instead she hovered about the table, looking me over.

I noticed that when I was around her she gave off no mind energy. I didn't pick up any fragments of thoughts and her emotions were completely shut off to me. Her body language, however, spoke volumes. There was fear and along with the fear a pure hatred. Was it that she couldn't understand me and feared the unknown? Or had she seen something about me that made her anticipate trouble?

I tried a weak attempt at entering her mind about a week after I had moved into the house. I'd left off work in the library and had come down to the kitchen in search of coffee. Claudine was engaged in a task and didn't notice me. I stood as close behind her as I dared and tried to penetrate her mind. I was instantly flung back and I backed into the scrubbed pine kitchen table. Claudine turned sharply to face me. Her eyes flashed and her lip curled in a sneer. She turned back to her chore. I grabbed a cup and managed to control my shaking hand enough to splash coffee into it. I retreated to the library.

After that incident I was glad to avoid Claudine whenever possible. I shut myself in the library and got on with my task. After all I had found a discreet and safe place to be. The books fed and comforted me. My task was engaging and the days passed pleasantly. I was sure that Stride wouldn't, couldn't, find me and I was out of sight. Why rock the boat? I didn't, after all, need company. I was used to being alone.

Gradually though the atmosphere in the house began to wear me down. I started to wonder what had really happened with my predecessor who was so briefly mentioned. Was it simply that he found living alongside Claudine too much to bear? Or had he ignored Claudine's injunctions to stay away from Miss Greta? Had he left of his own accord or been chased away?

Alone in my apartment I began to make elaborate speculations as to the fate of my predecessor. I started to see Claudine as a witch or sorceress. She had all the airs of some gris-gris woman from the bayous. When the dreams started, it was then that I had to take myself in hand and make a determined effort to supress the workings of my over-fevered imagination.

It was inevitable, looking back, that a crisis should be reached.

I had endured another silent meal under the cold scrutiny of Claudine. I watched her out of the corner of my eye. It looked exactly as if she were casting an evil eye on me. The comparison to a gris-gris woman came back into my mind with savage force.

I pushed back from the table and confronted her.

'You must know me well enough by now. Can't you stop watching me? You're like a cat with a mouse.'

'I know what you are. I've seen it. You and the books. They're more than just books to you.'

'I'm not interested in the books.'

'Yes you are. And it's unnatural. I know what you are.'

Again she flashed me a look of pure malevolence with her eyes like a cat.

'Look, I don't know…' I started to protest.

'But I do. I know exactly what you're after and you better keep your hands off.'

'Look – I'm just doing what I'm paid for. I'm not going to steal the books if that's what you're getting at.'

'I don't give a damn about the books. I know what you're really after. I got to watch you. Make sure you stay away.'

'I don't know what you're talking about.'

'You keep away from Miss Greta. I told you she's mine. And don't go fooling yourself that I don't know what you really are,' she screamed at me.

I had to get out of there. Get away from her.

Back in my rooms I tried to make sense of her savage outburst. That she should be protective of Greta made sense but what threat had Claudine detected in me? There was no way she could really understand my true nature. I'd given no signs. Or had I?

I scrutinised the time I'd been in the Plantation House in my mind's eye. Nothing. Maybe the woman was just obsessive. Any interloper would be welcomed with the same treatment.

The fact was I wanted it to be like that. I wanted to be above suspicion. I wanted to be left in peace.

For an hour or so I made up my mind. I'd have to leave. I couldn't take much more of Claudine. And what if she had somehow guessed at what I was like. I knew I had to get out. I started to get my things together.

Then the rational side of my mind took over. How could she possibly know what I really was? So, I loved books. So what? There was no way in hell she could possibly conceive of what I really was. I was safe here. Safe from Stride. What could Claudine do to me? Make life unpleasant?

I was going to stay; stay where I was safe. Claudine would just have to suck it up. I told myself that I was stronger than her.

CHAPTER FIFTEEN

I knew that it was only a matter of time before I would need to feed properly. I also knew that I would have to hunt a good distance away from my sanctuary. It stood to reason that Greta and Claudine were totally off limits.

I made my preparations and scouted my hunting ground. I timed the night of the hunt to just before I expected the real hunger to set in and incapacitate me beyond bearing and force me into some sort of reckless action.

The storm broke in the early afternoon and by nightfall sheets of rain were lashing against the house. The driveway was awash and when I got down on to the highway it was already running like a river. There was no way I was going anywhere that night. A night drive of a hundred miles or more was out of the question. Running back into the house was enough to ensure I was properly drenched. I consoled myself with the thought that nobody would be out on the streets on a night such as this.

Back in the house I changed out of my soaking clothes. I sat down to watch a show on the TV in my room. I had miscalculated. The first signs of the hunger manifested themselves after just a few minutes.

I dragged myself to the library. The books soothed the pangs of the hunger for a while. Then it was back in full fury. I was pushed beyond rational thought. I had to find the closest available nourishment before I was completely overcome. I was a ravening beast, driven by instinct.

I knew where to find prey. There was no thought of the consequences as barefoot I prowled the darkened corridors. On the lower floor I made out a sliver of dim light leaking around a slightly open door. Greta's bedroom.

I knew she would already be deep in a drug induced sleep. I approached the room without making a sound, hugging the walls to ensure the floorboards didn't creek.

Inside the room a night light cast a soft glow into the room. As expected, Greta was huddled under the covers, breathing gently and fast asleep. What I was not expecting was the figure of Claudine seated at the bedside. It looked to me like she too was deep asleep.

I could enter Greta's mind, feed and slip away without waking Claudine as long as there was no disturbance when I left my body. There was a window seat across from the bed and I made sure that my body was lying on it securely before I reached out and entered Greta's mind.

At once I was confronted by a figure, outlined against the rose-golden glow of my objective; Greta's vital essence. It was there but tantalisingly just out of reach. I had to get past the figure that was approaching before I could feed. The figure came closer.

It was Claudine. She looked at me coldly, her jaw set, her dark brown eyes boring into my soul. She seemed larger somehow, imposing and full of strength.

'I knew you'd get here sooner or later. Wouldn't be able to help yourself.'

I was stunned as it dawned on me that here was another being that was like me. I was both stunned and intimidated.

'I've been watching you.' Her voice was full of menace but her tone was flat and void of emotion. 'You have all the signs.'

I stood there dumbly and began to tremble. The hunger was asserting itself again.

'This is my turf. Greta is mine. Stay away.'

The hunger made me braver. I moved forward as if to push past Claudine. It was the simple motion of her hand that pushed me back and laid me on my back. She didn't even need to touch me. She seemed to radiate a fearful power.

'I'm stronger than you and I have fed. I'm older too. Wiser.'

I curled in a foetal ball and whimpered.

'How long?'

I groaned incomprehension.

'How long since you fed?'

I forced a response.

'I'll let you feed if you promise to do exactly as I say. I don't want my property damaged. You haven't been changed long have you?'

She must have taken my whimpering for agreement to both her propositions. She dragged me erect. Her strength was beyond her image.

I leaned on her like an invalid as she helped me to approach the gently glowing mass of Greta's mental energy.

'Feed but when I tell you, you must stop. Take it gently. Feed carefully.'

I began to gulp in Greta's energy and was pulled back sharply.

'I said carefully. Sip.'

I obeyed and felt the pangs of the hunger subside. Claudine did not let me continue as I would have liked. She jerked me away from the feast just as the griping hunger pangs left me.

'That's enough. You've had enough. First lesson – control yourself. Leave your prey enough to survive you.'

I was calmer now, now that the driving force of the hunger no longer blotted out the rational being inside me. What Claudine said made sense to me. I felt good, not bloated and guilt laden, but energised and remade. She was wise.

'We need to talk. Come on.'

Claudine dragged me from Greta's mind and we reclaimed our bodies.

We sat at the kitchen table. Claudine had made coffee.

'When and how?'

It was relief to tell the story from beginning to end. It all tumbled out of me. Petersen's death, Betty Petersen and all the others. And finally Detective Lieutenant Stride.

I felt lighter; especially as I knew that Claudine must understand. She was the same. She already knew the feelings and the guilt. She already must know what it was like to hide your true nature and the alienation that came with it.

'You had no one? What about your momma?'

I told her about my childhood. The fact that I never really knew my parents or what had happened to them. I told her about my supposed Aunt and Uncle. I ventured a question of my own.

'When did you know? What you are?'

'My momma called it mindworm. That what she said we were, mindworms.'

So I too was a mindworm. Somehow giving what I had become a name made me feel easier. It was like when a doctor gives a name to what's ailing you.

'Your mother too?'

'And my daddy.'

'They taught you? Taught you how to survive?'

'Uh huh. There's a way of living. A way to avoid trouble. You got your first lesson tonight. I can show you how to feed and not kill your prey, let them recover and go back for more.'

'Like you and Greta?'

'I've got something special planned for Greta. She's not just a source of nourishment. I want her body.'

I didn't have to speak. My incredulity and all the questions were written on my face.

'Yeah, you heard right. I want her body and I want her life.'

'But she's a sick woman,' I protested. 'She's dying if I'm any judge. Why change places with someone who can barely walk most days.'

'She's not that sick. Don't you get it? I'm making her sick. If you feed off someone they get weak. I let her recover just enough to keep her alive and then feed again. That's why you have to stay away.'

‘Why would you want her body anyway? You’re an attractive woman. You’re a smart woman.’

‘I’m a black woman.’

I had to yield to her logic.

‘And I wasn’t always a pretty woman.’

‘You...’

‘Oh yeah. I was a fat, plain black girl back then. That was when I was Donna. After I became Claudine – then I became a pretty woman. After I worked my way through college, then I became a smart, pretty woman’

‘You’ve taken...’

‘Someone’s body and their life. Yes I’ve done that.’

‘And now you want to be Greta?’

‘Seems a good move. I made some mistakes back then, but you learn from experience. Seems that a plain black woman’s more acceptable than a pretty black woman and a smart, pretty black woman is not acceptable at all.’

‘Why not just take what you need? You seem to have it all figured out.’

‘It’s not that easy. You need to form a bond with...well with your new self. That’s what I’ve been working on all these months. Greta relies on me. We’re close now...almost like kin.’

We were silent then. It was all a lot to take in and understand. Then Claudine broke the silence,

'So, now you know to stay away from my Greta. Here's the deal. I can see you need help – you need a momma or at least a friend. I'll help you, show you what you can do and what you must not. I'll hunt with you and keep you clear of trouble. Then when the time comes Greta's all mine. Deal?'

So Claudine became my momma and life was good.

CHAPTER SIXTEEN

'You know you almost had me convinced back there. You had me thinking that you were just some poor stiff who was always in the wrong place through no fault of his own. Then you ran and I just knew there was something in it.'

It was Stride and he was standing right behind me.

I thought I had turned my life around. I had companionship of a sort with someone who understood and shared my strange appetite. Thanks to Claudine I had learned to hunt and feed without drawing attention to myself. She had taught me how to listen to the buzzing of emotions and thoughts that came to me from all around me when I was with people. I could hear them clearly now. I had a safe place and pleasant employment. And now my arch nemesis was back and close enough to reach out a hand and touch me.

'Have you come to take me back? Like a Texas Ranger? Dead or alive?'

Stride grinned.

'I'm not a cop anymore.'

'Really? How come?'

'I retired. Handed in my papers and walked away.'

'And you've just come to look up an old friend. I don't buy it.'

'I'm just a concerned citizen now. I'm making you my retirement project.'

'More like it. You're here to stay then?'

'For the foreseeable future. I've got a room over in the Colonial House. Very pleasant. C'mon, I'll spring for lunch. We should catch up.'

This was a different Stride alright. Maybe this was some sort of ploy to take me off my guard. He seemed relaxed, outgoing, less razor sharp than before.

I followed him across the street and we took a table in the conservatory at the back of the restaurant. The lunch time crowd hadn't come in yet and we had the room to ourselves. We ordered and while we waited we faced each other across the white expanse of the tablc cloth.

'So what's all this about retirement?'

'I got tired of all the B-S. The rules, the regulations and keeping thc Councilmen sweet.'

'And being told who to investigate? What cases to drop?'

'That too.'

'I see you kept your sidearm.' I couldn't help noticing the police special that nestled under his jacket.

‘I didn’t think that they’d grudge a twenty-five year man a little souvenir.’

‘You planning to use it any time soon?’

‘It’s just a habit. Strap it on each morning, just like always.’

‘I wouldn’t fancy a bullet in my back.’

‘You’re safe with me. I know what you did. But I need to know how. I’m curious. If you’re dead you can’t tell me. But you will...sometime.’

Our order came then and we ate in silence for a while.

‘They opened her up you know?’

‘Who?’

‘Your girl-friend Patsy-Anne.’

‘She wasn’t...’

‘Your girl-friend. You said...at the time. Still I’m surprised you’d forgotten her already. Or is it that there have been others? Since.’

I didn’t dignify that with a response.

‘Anyhow – Patsy-Anne. They did a full autopsy. After you’d left town. They opened up her skull. Know what they found?’

‘How should I?’

‘Part of her brain was missing. No, that’s not strictly accurate. Parts of it had turned to a grey jelly mush. Nobody can figure out what happened but they reckon that’s what killed her.’

'And you think it was something I did?'

'If not you, then who?'

'Or what? She could have been sick. A brain disease. Did they autopsy the Petersen's?'

'No. They were buried and no one was going to dig them up. I tried but my Captain…you know.'

I nodded my understanding. It was like we were two colleagues discussing a past experience not hunter and quarry. I could see where this was going and put up my guard.

'How did you find me? Down here?'

'Simple enough. You made a mistake and used a credit card to pay for your room at the Colonial House. It popped up on the watch list I'd set up.'

'Even though it wasn't an official case…'

'You make friends as you go along. Call in favours.'

'And here you are.'

'You'd managed to stay low before that – must have paid cash up until then. Still everybody makes a mistake from time to time. Then you got rid of the Volvo. Big mistake and not necessary. Plenty of Volvo's about. Me, I've always driven American but plenty of people choose not to. It came up on the vehicle licensing database. Another friend.'

We'd finished eating by then. Stride pushed his plate away and sparked up a cigarette.

'Like they say, you can run but you can't hide. Disappearing takes a lot of hard work and you just don't have the smarts.'

'So – you still have no case against me. You were right when you said I just happened to be in the wrong place when three people I knew all died. I'm an innocent here.'

'You want me to think that you're some sort of Jonah. You bring bad luck to those you touch...'

'Just those three...that's all it's been.'

'Three I can put you with.'

'There are no others.'

'I've got a theory about you. Want to hear it.'

'You bought lunch. I'll listen.'

'I don't think you like yourself or what you've done. Something drives you to it...some appetite for slaughter. But after, that's when the regret starts tearing you apart. I think you want to confess, get it off your soul. You don't understand what's driving you. You want to be helped. I'm going to stick close because when you are ready to spill I want to be the one you spill too.'

I forced a laugh. Stride was getting too close to the real situation. He pushed back his chair and picked up his hat.

'You can count on seeing a lot more of me. And even when you don't see me don't be fooled that

I'm not close by with eyes on you. You'll slip up and I'll be there. Then I'll have you. Think about it. I'll listen to your real story. I'll hear your confession. You'll feel better after it. Check's taken care of.'

He dug in a pocket and handed over a business card.

'My cell number. Call me anytime if you have something to say. Be seeing you.'

He was still a cop. You don't slough off twenty-five years just like that. The little scene we'd just played out was to lull me and create some sort of bond that he could use. He was smart; a clever and deadly adversary. Whether he had a badge or not didn't matter. He was here to bring me down. I was in deep trouble.

CHAPTER SEVENTEEN

Now though I was not alone. I had a mentor. I had Claudine. I took my story to her.

By the time I got back to the Plantation House I was a quivering wreck and almost incoherent. Claudine served me coffee at the kitchen table that had become our venue of choice when things needed discussion. It had been my schoolroom as she explained the lore and logic of my new form. My mindworm form. It had been where she had scolded when I had ignored her advice. It had been a place of companionship and safety.

When I had finally pulled myself together I told her of my encounter with Stride. She seemed unfazed by this new development.

'So what can he do? Now you know how to live right there'll be nothing for him to find out. Just keep clean and he'll go away.'

'You don't know him. He's like a dog with a bone. He's obsessed with me.'

'So let him obsess.'

'He still has his sidearm. When he can't pin anything on me he'll get itchy. I can't live with waiting for a bullet in my back.'

'Ah. Like that huh?'

I didn't realise that I was going to say it but it came out anyway.

'And I'm concerned for you. He'll be close all the time. He might get in the way when you...with Greta.'

'You mean when I take her. I can see the problem. I'm touched by your concern.'

We sat in silence. I could see that Claudine was working something in her mind. She still remained shut off from me so I couldn't pick up her thought fragments but I could still tell by the look of intense concentration on her face.

'There might be a way.'

'Yes?'

'You could take Stride's body. Then he'd be gone and you'd be free and clear.'

'Could I do that?'

'I've done it. I've told you. I'm all set to do it again. I could show you how.'

'But you said you needed to be close to your chosen...what?'

'Host – let's call it that. Yes, there needs to be a bond. Doesn't come easy.'

'Me and Stride? Really? Never going to happen.'

'It's happened already. You two are getting like an old married couple. Trust me. He needs you and now you need him. Could you live in him? Even for a while?'

I thought about that. It seemed like I didn't have much choice. I told Claudine that it would be tolerable.

'Pity you can't always choose your host. Circumstances dictate. Sometimes you make a bad choice for what seem all the right reasons.'

The way she said it made me ask without thinking,

'That happened to you?'

'Made it obvious huh? Claudine was my best friend. You know, pretty girl and plain girl. I envied her looks. It was more than that though. I wanted Duane her man. I made a bad choice there. There were things about Duane that I didn't know, hadn't seen from the outside looking in.'

'But now you're here? What happened?'

'In the end it was him or me. I sucked him dry and left him by the roadside back in Alabama. I don't suppose them that found him paid much attention. No one came after me but then we weren't married or anything like that. He was just another unexplained dead black man. I took myself off to college – Claudine was always a clever girl. I worked my way through. Got what I thought I needed and set out to conquer the world. Doesn't always work out the way you think it will.'

‘And you can show me the way?’

‘To take someone’s body? To take over someone’s life? Sure. The secret is to take them to the point of death. Lead them up to the big door but don’t knock. Just before that death tremor kicks off, you pull them back and hold on. That’s when they struggle. That’s when you need to be strong. You hold on until they lose the will to struggle and then they accept. They move away, head off to parts unknown and leave you in possession.’

‘Not that easy then.’

‘I did it. You can too. Depends on how much you want to survive.’

I had a lot to think about. There was a way out but it was going to take nerve and strength. I was pretty sure that in such a struggle Stride would cling to life tenaciously. I wondered how I would stand up in a life or death contest.

I went off to the library and sought peace and calm with the books. I sat and thought.

I put off making a decision. I would always tell myself that tomorrow would be a good time. I knew I would eventually run out of tomorrows. I told myself that if I acted quickly I could control the situation. Every day of delay edged that control a little further out of my grasp.

A week passed and then another. I went back to Claudine. She told me again and again how it could be accomplished. Still I delayed. It was a big question. Was I ready to live? Was I ready to control the future? Was I ready to risk it all or would I wait until some other force overwhelmed me?

CHAPTER EIGHTEEN

Although Claudine's plan made a lot of sense I still held back. Despite my needs I was still a moral being. I clung to the ethics of a civilized man. Now that I had learned how to feed without killing how could I kill to save my own skin?

That's what it would be. Taking Stride's body would be murder. His spirit or soul or whatever made him a living, breathing entity would be banished to who knows where. To oblivion most likely. It would be murder. Cold blooded and calculated. Murder!

'I can't do it.' I told Claudine after two weeks had gone by.

'It's up to you. It's easy to have fine moral scruples when you're safe and warm and well fed. But let me remind you that your safety is a fragile thing. I'm not about to let protecting you get in the way of what I need. There'll be consequences for you then.'

I looked at her dumbly but there was a chill in her words and up my spine.

'I can see you get it. Greta's ripe and I'm going to pluck her. It'll be any day now. When I do you'll have another corpse to explain to Detective Stride when he comes calling. And you know he will come calling. Of course I could help you out.

I could suck him dry. Then there'd be another corpse to explain. To the County Sheriff and his friends this time. The longer the list the more the finger points to you. Then they'll really start to look at you. And it will be official this time. Not just one man with an obsession.'

She motioned for me to sit. She poured coffee. She was going to try to reason with me. First the threat then the balm. I sat stiffly.

'Look, you still think of what you are as an affliction. I look at it another way. It's evolution. You must have read Darwin when you've been wallowing in all those books in that college library of yours.'

I nodded agreement. I could see where her argument was going.

'You think we're some superior manifestation of the race. Is that it? That's your argument?'

'It's as good as any I've ever heard. Whatever we are, that's the way we are. The prime directive that's built into us is to survive. Survive by whatever means we have to use.'

I shook my head. I couldn't accept the argument however attractive it might be. I couldn't deprive Stride of his being in cold blood. The others had been accidents and misadventures before I had learned how to control what I was; affliction or gift. Claudine gave it one last try.

'Listen to me. Does the fox think about the welfare of the chickens when he devours them? Do wolves debate what is best for the caribou they chase down? Did you spare a thought for the donor of that fine steak I cooked for you this evening? Of course you didn't! It's about survival. Your scruples are a luxury you can't afford.'

In the end it was Stride himself who made the telling argument. As we sat there in the kitchen, the coffee cooling between us, the doorbell cut the silence. Claudine went to answer it and her call summoned me.

Stride was standing in the doorway. Claudine slipped away but I knew she must be within earshot and listening. He grinned maliciously and gave me a 'Good afternoon'

'I thought I'd drop by. Wouldn't want you thinking I'd forgotten you,' and he slipped past me into the hallway.

He'd crossed the line. He'd invaded my territory. He'd sent me a signal. Claudine's remarks about the fragility of safety echoed in my mind. I could almost feel the bullet cleaving my flesh.

Stride was already heading down the hallway.

‘Another nice place you’ve found for yourself. Does the lady look after you OK?’ His voice was insinuating, smooth.

I followed him. Grabbed at him. He avoided me.

‘Where do you get to sleep? Up here?’ as he mounted the stairs.

I finally managed to get a grip on him and spun him around.

‘You’ve got no right…’ I began.

His sneer cut me short. ‘Can’t I visit with an old acquaintance?’

‘Leave me alone.’

‘Or what?’

‘Leave now.’

Stride held out his palms in a gesture of surrender. His smile was one of triumph. He’d scored some points. He’d made me lose my patience and react to the intrusion. He didn’t need to push it further. Not this time. He had all the time in the world.

He turned and left without another word. He didn’t go far though. He sat in his car just at the top of the drive and stared at me coolly. He was taunting me. Inviting me to engage further. I seethed inside but made myself hold back.

He lighted a cigarette and drew on it deeply. He blew a long plume of smoke out of the open window. After long minutes he waved a hand, started the engine and made for the highway.

Back in the hallway Claudine emerged from the shadows. We exchanged looks pregnant with meaning. No words were needed. It was sealed.

CHAPTER NINETEEN

It was my turn to surprise Lieutenant Stride. I used the number he had given me and placed a call to his cell phone.

There was a brief silence when I announced myself. I thought I heard a sharp intake of breath. Then,

'What can I do for you?'

'I'm ready. You were right. It's got too much for me. I want it to be over. I'll tell you the whole story.'

'I'm sensing there's a catch. You'll tell all to me if. What's the if?'

'I want you to promise that you'll take me in and make sure I get treatment. I'm remembering your service revolver. You've still got it. When you've had your curiosity satisfied what's to stop you gunning me down.'

'You'll have to trust me won't you? But sure – if you come quietly I won't want your life. It's not revenge it's about justice.'

'You know I think I believe you. Ok meet me this evening...'

When I laid out the meeting place for him Stride was not happy but I explained that I wanted somewhere we couldn't be disturbed and he agreed to go along with it. I'd counted on him being eager to get what he had been pursuing so hard and I got the result I wanted.

'Come alone.' I warned. 'I don't want the place swarming with cops.'

'This isn't True Detective and I'm not a cop anymore. There is only me.'

I named the meeting time and hung up.

In the grounds of the Plantation House but at some distance from the big house there was a plot of land set aside for the family cemetery. It was the model of a country churchyard, with a small chapel, some weathered gravestones and the family mausoleum that held the bodies of Greta's dead husband and his parents. This was the meeting place I had selected for my showdown with Stride.

The cemetery was surrounded by a low wall and was screened from the main house by a stand of mature white oaks. It was set on top of a rise of ground and thus had a perfect view of the open grassland of the estate and the road that led from the main highway up to the house.

As I had planned I took up a position outside the chapel just as the evening light was fading to a twilight gloom. I could see perfectly well but in less than an hour the night would have brought on pitch darkness.

I saw Stride's car turn off of the highway and approach the house. He was right on time. I could only guess at his eagerness to confront me and to hear my story. He must have been bursting with delight at getting what he had so long desired.

Scanning the open ground I was sure that nobody was with him. He was alone as he came up the packed earth path through the trees and came into the cemetery. Finally we came face to face. I could see that he was still carrying the pistol in the shoulder holster.

'Good evening Lieutenant. You're punctual. Please can I trouble you to take out the gun carefully and put it on the tombstone over there,' and I pointed out a large, flat stone memorial a few yards away.

Although he didn't seem to like it Stride pulled out the gun between finger and thumb and placed it where I had indicated. He came back to his spot opposite me.

'It's chilly out here. I hope this is going to be worthwhile.'

'Lieutenant, I promised you the truth. That's what you are going to hear.'

So I told him my story. I told him about Tom Petersen and his heart attack. I told him about Betty and her desire to depart her sad existence.

Patsy-Anne's story was told too and then the others were all spoken of in their rightful order. When I'd finished I stood there waiting in silence for Stride's response.

He smirked and shook his head.

'You left out the bit about being bitten by a radioactive spider. Which comic book did you get all that from?'

It was then that I lost control. Didn't Stride realise what the confession had cost me? Couldn't he see the truth in what I was saying? I leaped into his mind and fought hard against my inclination to devour the man's essence and remove him in a frenzy of feeding.

I pulled myself together and immersed myself in the golden glow of his energy. With measured steps I began to feed, consuming Stride's vitality slowly and inexorably.

As I felt the death shudder about to erupt I stopped feeding and braced myself. The final tremor never came and I felt myself being forced from Stride's mind. I pushed back and held my ground. Then I could hear Stride's mind begin to howl in agony and rage as he fought back at me. I focussed my mind energy at this aggression and fought it back until I saw the force glowing in one corner of Stride's mind space.

I threw myself at the hot whiteness of this ball of energy and forced my own mind to combine with it.

I felt a pulsing tremor and I knew that Stride, or the thought energy that was Stride, was leaving, and disappearing into the ether. In my mind I suddenly had a vision of the man. He looked back at me and the grin on his face was one of triumph as well as resolution. He was telling me that he had scored some sort of victory and was leaving content.

When my vision cleared I knew that I was seeing through Stride's eyes. At my feet I could see the crumpled form of my own former self. I had acquired Stride's body and banished his spirit to who knew where.

I looked down at myself or what had once been me. The face was the same face I'd seen in the mirror every morning. The eyes were still open but there was nothing there. I was looking at an empty dwelling. I bent down and closed the staring eyes.

The slight figure on the ground already looked to be shrunken as if it were decaying as I looked on. I felt a rush of revulsion and turned away.

I tried to process what I had done. I was in Stride's body. I had taken over his form. But was I Stride? How much of me, the librarian, the insignificant and lonely man remained? How much of what I now was, was Stride?

I saw a white clad figure coming towards me from the trees. What had brought Greta here?

'Greta? Is that you? What are you doing here?'

'Yes, it's me. Who else? And what am I doing here? I live here. What are you doing? Who the hell are you and what have you done to my librarian?'

This was Greta alright. But a stronger and more forceful version. The vapid woman had been replaced by a determined and assertive copy. I was stunned.

Then Greta's face broke into mirth and a deep booming laugh erupted from the thin body.

'Claudine? Is it you? What's going on?'

'I thought it was the right time for a double event. I'd planned it and now was a good time. No – it was the best time. I see you handled your situation satisfactorily. So this is Lieutenant Stride. Not much of an improvement if you don't mind me saying.'

She was obviously in great good humour. She'd got what she wanted. I didn't mind her comment either. I was safe and a new life without the troublesome interference of Lieutenant Stride was opening up before me.

'We've still got work to do,' Greta/Claudine brought me back to reality.

I hadn't thought beyond the act of taking over Stride's body. Now there was the lifeless corpse of the being I had once been lying on the ground, out in the open. I supposed that somewhere in the big house the husk that Claudine had once inhabited was also stretched out.

'In the family mausoleum,' and Greta produced a key.

We gathered my discarded body up and dumped it in the tomb alongside the effigies of Greta's husband and his forbears.

I accompanied Greta back to the house and retrieved Claudine's remnants and transported them back up the slight rise and placed them alongside my own remains. Greta locked the thick ornamental doors and all evidence of our night's work was safely out of sight.

In the moonlight I noticed the glint of blue-black metal. I scooped up Stride's weapon and stowed it back in the shoulder holster.

Back in the house Greta made tea and we sat in the kitchen.

'What now?'

'I supposed that you'd want to light out for pastures new. You can't hang around here anyway. An ex-policeman would start to look out of place. And you need to start being ex-Detective Stride. Did you have another name by the way?'

It was there without thinking, 'John. He was John Stride.'

'Great, you are John Stride. So, John Stride you'd better get into your car and get back to your hotel.'

'And you?'

'I'm right where I want to be. I've got just what I was wanting. I'm going to enjoy it for a while – see what develops. Maybe, one day, I'll try to get back to the movies. If you see I'm in a new picture sometime you go and see it.'

'But how will you explain our disappearance? Claudine and me? The old me?'

'Won't be any explaining to do. People like you and me don't draw attention. We come and go and nobody cares. We don't count for anything. Anybody cares to ask I'll just say you got tired of my company the two of you and went off to find something more conducive.'

I knew she was right. And I knew that I was on my own again.

CHAPTER TWENTY

I climbed behind the wheel of Stride's car and headed back into town.

I parked in the parking lot behind the hotel and entered the lobby. I had almost reached the staircase leading up to the rooms when a voice hailed me. I hadn't internalised the idea that I was now Mr Stride and had my foot on the first step when:

'Mr Stride...good evening. Don't forget your key.'

It was the owner, a pleasant woman of about fifty-five. She was right behind me holding out a key with a heavy metal tag attached to it. I feigned coming out of an absent minded study, gave her a smile and took the offered key from her.

'It's nice to see you Mr Stride. I was wondering how your business here in town was progressing.'

I had no idea what Stride had told her about his purpose in visiting the town but I read the subtext of the enquiry. How long was I planning to stay?

I had already concluded on the drive back into town that leaving straight away might prove suspicious if anybody also remarked the disappearance of Claudine and my now defunct self.

'Things are coming together I'm glad to say but I expect to be around for a few more days yet. Will that be convenient for you?'

'It's a genuine pleasure to have you here John. You're welcome as long as you want to stay. I hope you're finding it all to your liking here.'

I didn't like that 'John' that came out of nowhere. Had Stride started something that might complicate my life? Was the complication just about to start?

I assured the owner of the Plantation House that I was enjoying my stay and that everything was indeed how I would want it. Then I climbed the stairs two at a time and reached the safety of my room.

I had to be alone and start to gather up the pieces of my new identity. I was hoping that Stride would have left me some clues up here in his hotel room.

The tinnitus of emotions and thought fragments was back inside my head. They were leaking through the partition walls that formed the room as my fellow guests went about their business. I would miss the solitude of the Plantation House.

Stride was a tidy man. He had a single suitcase with a few shirts and pieces of underwear inside. The rest of his clothes, shirts, a second dark suit, socks and underwear had been neatly stowed in the wardrobe and dresser drawers. It seemed that Stride was not fond of casual clothes.

There was a briefcase on the bed and I flipped it open and drew out a sheaf of papers. I settled in the armchair that stood beside the bed. Along with the contents of his wallet, I started to study the documents.

There was a letter from the police department and signed by the Captain of Detectives, congratulating Lieutenant Stride on his retirement after twenty-five years of service. So that much of Stride's story was true. It looked also that he had severed his ties with our town back in New England. There was a receipt for the keys of his apartment and for a final payment of rent.

I looked through the wallet. There were a couple of credit cards and an ATM card. I riffled through the papers from the briefcase and found a bank statement. At least Stride was solvent.

Back in the wallet I dug out his driver's license and his gun permit. The gun would have to go and soon.

There were no photographs in the wallet or among the papers. It looked very much like Stride, like me, was a loner. No wife, no children, no parents. Therefore, if I avoided our home town I'd never meet anyone who knew Stride intimately and who might want to share memories of which I was unaware.

Without my noticing a cigarette had found its way into my hand and was now half smoked. I ground it out in the ashtray. This was a habit I would have to ditch along with the gun. A pack with five cigarettes was on the bedside table alongside a lighter. It was a commonplace object. I turned it over in my hand; no monogram, nothing to indicate a connection with anyone.

I felt like I could use a drink. I went straight to the bedside cabinet and took out a half-filled bottle of bourbon. I held it in my hand and then replaced it. I wanted a drink but I also wanted to be among people. I checked the bedside clock. It was still reasonably early. The bar along the street from the Colonial House would still be open.

In the bar I ordered a beer and a shot of bourbon and took a seat in a booth from where I could scan the room. Without thinking I lit a cigarette.

Sitting with my half empty glass I started to become aware of thoughts, Stride's thoughts, forming in my mind. It was like awakening from a temporary amnesia. I was starting to bond with my new form and meld my identity with what remained of Stride.

Then, like a dam bursting, Stride's thoughts and memories flooded back and joined my own awareness. I had been right. Stride was a loner just like me. He was an obsessive and like a terrier would not let go of anything he got his jaws wrapped around. He was a good cop, a smart investigator. And mercifully he was alone. No wife. There never had been. No kids. Parents gone. No friends.

It occurred to me that in me he had found the whole purpose for his life. If he had managed to bring me to justice then he would really be on his own. A tear of self-pity trickled and I tossed back the bourbon.

I let things lie for a couple of days. I visited the library just to see my suet dumpling friend and take some energy from the books. I shopped for some more clothes; something a bit less formal than Stride's dark suits. I visited a couple of bars and observed the street life.

It was coming time for me to leave and I had some unfinished business back at the Plantation House. I drove out there.

First of all I had to take care of my car. If I was to disappear then the car would need to disappear too. It was an irony that the only footprint I had left on the face of the earth was a car.

I needn't have worried. Greta had taken care of things. Alongside the main house there was a coach house which had stayed locked up all the time I had been living there. Inside was a collection of vintage automobiles, assembled over the years by the family. Greta had moved my car and Claudine's in among the Bentley's, Rolls Royce and the Cadillacs. It was perfect hiding in plain sight.

I gathered up Tom Petersen's books and stowed them in the trunk of Stride's car. They had served me well and I'd probably need their aid and comfort in the future. It was one link with my past form that I could never abandon. I was tempted to help myself to the Gutenberg bible but decided that that was a step too far. There was a nice edition of 'Tristram Shandy' though and I did add that to Petersen's hoard. A memento. Why not?

I was tempted to visit the mausoleum and to take one last look at what I had been. What was the point of looking at an empty shell, I argued with myself. It would be best to let that part of what I was decay undisturbed and embrace my new opportunities.

Greta and I had a brief farewell. We would never meet again. That tore at me briefly. I had become used to having the comfort of a fellow being who knew what was really happening to me. It was good too to have a mentor and Claudine had guided me in my darkest times. Now I was alone again.

I climbed back behind the wheel of Stride's car and headed off without too much of a plan. I'd leave it to fate, karma and even serendipity.

Now I was John Stride.

CHAPTER TWENTY-ONE

I sat in the outer office of the doctor's surgery while the nurse made appointments for my treatment.

I had noticed the cough almost as soon as I had taken over Stride's body but had thought nothing of it. It had become worse as the weeks went by, deep and hacking, wracking the bony frame with spasms. When the chest pains kicked in, at first I was in denial, living on a diet of pharmacy pain-killers and black coffee.

When I eventually dragged myself to the doctor's office I knew it would not be good news. Behind the sympathetic smile and the assurance that he and the hospital would do their best I read a sense of regret. There was no hope beyond a miracle.

When I asked the direct question, 'How long?' the doctor turned away unable to look me in the eye. The poor man must have been in this situation too many times. He mumbled a formulaic response and invited me to go sit in the outer office. The nurse would take care of the necessary arrangements.

Back on the street I needed a cigarette. It was just one of the habits I had picked up when I acquired Stride's body. I joined the other pariahs gathered around the street door of the office building. I dragged on the cigarette sucking soothing nicotine into my lungs.

It was small comfort to realise that I hadn't had much choice in selecting my new host. It had after all been an emergency situation. Given time I would have been more careful and not selected a body with so many defects.

As it turned out detective Stride had lied to me. He hadn't chosen to retire from the police; his illness had forced the decision on him. Nevertheless he had decided to dedicate his last few months to hunting me down. It certainly said something about his obsession with me or of his desire to unravel the puzzle that pricked at him.

The immediate craving satisfied I went looking for a bar. It was another of Stride's quirks that I had inherited. While I found ease in a library Stride's habitat of choice was a bar, the seedier the better. It also became apparent that his choice of nourishment, chain smoked cigarettes apart, was beer and an occasional shot of cheap bourbon whisky. Given the chance Stride would sit for hours in a booth at the back of a bar feeding on the snippets of conversation around him and sipping from a tall glass.

I found a place at the back of a bar that was two blocks over from the doctor's office. I slid into the booth with my glass and cursed my luck. I had just been handed a death sentence.

I drank and thought. There were no distractions as the place was empty. At this hour the television behind the bar was turned off and the barman was busy with getting ready for the lunch time rush.

Strangely I felt a wave of relief. I just had to wait and let the disease take its course and I would be released from my burden. The hunger would be gone. The feeding frenzy would be no more. I wouldn't be impelled to kill in order to survive. Make no mistake, I still had not come to terms with my nature and the things I was driven to do.

I drained my glass and signalled for a refill. It took just the time for the barman to draw the beer and bring the glass over to me for the drive for survival inherent in all nature to surface in me.

I did not want to die. No matter how badly I thought about myself and what I needed to do, it was preferable to oblivion. I had had what I had become thrust upon me. It was not my fault. Maybe it was an accident of birth. Who knew and who cared? Not me. I was becoming defiant. Something of Stride's mulish character had entered me when I took his body. The alcohol only served to strengthen its hold. I was not going to lie back and let this disease take me. I was going to fight.

Then it dawned on me. I didn't need to stand and fight. I could run away.

I'd acquired Stride's body with all its defects to get me out of a bad situation. I could find another, more suitable to my needs, and take that and let the husk that had been Stride crumble to dust.

Frankly I was finding Stride irksome. I did not want to spend my time hanging out with low lifes in dark depressing bars. I hated the smoking and the paroxysms of coughing which came after every nicotine laden drag. I hated his attitudes and his appalling habits. I'd be glad to be rid of Stride.

I could see it clearly now, the way forward, the way to my salvation. Someone else would have to yield up their place but what did that matter. Survival of the fittest!

This time though I would be careful in my selection. I'd take my time and make sure that the selected host conformed more closely to my requirements. I started to build a mental image of my ideal host.

My life so far had been drawn on narrow lines; at least until Tom Petersen had helped reveal my true nature. I had to admit that up until then I had not enjoyed the fruits of life. I was being offered a new beginning here.

So, a young body and a young mind would be required. Someone already endowed with success and a firm background from which to climb upwards. No point in giving myself disadvantages to overcome from the start. Healthy stock of course, that was essential.

The source of such material had been staring me in the face. The city I happened to be in had one of the best regarded universities in the country. Real Ivy League!

I downed the remains of my beer – Stride could never leave a half full glass behind him – and went straight over to the main campus. Where to start? Obvious. The library.

I knew what I was looking for. I had seen golden youth often enough in my own college precincts though nothing as highly charged as the minds and bodies that offered themselves under the dome of the reading room.

I spotted a likely candidate without too much trouble. He looked the part, well-groomed, study-partnered by an attractive brunette with bobbed hair and seemingly absorbed in some intellectual task.

I knew already that outward appearances could be deceptive. I was prepared to invest some time, however, to make sure of my choice. The hunt had begun.

I selected a book at random from the shelves and approached the empty seat beside the young man.

'Will I disturb you if I sit here?'

ABOUT THE AUTHOR

David Pollard is a teller of tales – playwright, writer of short stories and novels.

Among many other writers and influences he is an admirer of Robert Louis Stevenson – which is why he adopted Tusitala as his website identity – it being the name given to Stevenson by the Samoan people meaning 'Teller of Tales' David believes that 'Treasure Island' is one of the finest adventure stories ever written.

David's passion apart from writing is the theatre. In Hereford where he now lives he is active in the amateur dramatic world. He is both an actor and director. He is also organising chairman of the county drama festival.

You can stay in touch with all of David's activities through his website: www.thetusitala.co.uk.

You can also follow David on Twitter @dpollardauthor.

Dear Reader,

Thank you for reading 'Mindworm'. I do hope you enjoyed it and that you'll pass the book on to your reading friends.
If this story is to your taste I am sure you will enjoy my book, 'The Alienation of Ludovic Weiss', which is also available on Amazon.
Just to whet your appetite here is the first chapter for you to savour.
And don't forget you can keep up with all my writing and performance activities by going to my website: www.thetusitala.co.uk.
Best wishes
David Pollard

THE ALIENATION OF LUDOVIC WEISS

MONDAY

Cancer starts unobtrusively and with no fanfare. A rogue cell divides and divides again. A spot of blood appears where it is not expected. In just such a way the settled and comfortable life of Ludovic Weiss began to disintegrate.

Nobody likes Monday morning and Weiss was no exception. It was not that he found his employment particularly onerous. In fact he relished his position within the Compliance Department. He enjoyed the status it afforded him heartily. He valued the companionship of his work colleagues and he felt assured that his superiors held him in high regard. His workplace was like an extension to his home and his family.

No-one, however, wants to leave behind the pleasure and leisure of the weekend and embark on another week of attention to detail, meetings that have to be attended and ever present deadlines. This particular weekend had been especially pleasurable. The weather had been dry and autumnal with just a hint of the chill that presages winter.

On Saturday Weiss had shopped with his wife. After, they had lunched and then gone to the cinema. They were showing a double bill of American films noirs. It was a genre with a strong appeal for Weiss. He liked the use of black and white film and found the inevitability of a disastrous ending for the main protagonists oddly satisfying, almost cathartic. Lil remarked wryly, as she always did, that this simply showed the darker side of Weiss' soul.

On Sunday morning they had made love as usual. Afterwards Weiss lay beside Lil enjoying her warmth and her soft woman smells. Weiss made breakfast and they sat together leafing through the Sunday newspapers. Later they drove into the country and went to lunch with Lil's parents.

Weiss liked his in-laws and looked forward to the weekly visits. This was not least because he felt sure that both mother and father respected and liked him in their turn. They showed him the due deference that came with his rise within the Department. In one memorable moment, when a considerable amount of wine had flowed, Lil's father had actually complimented Weiss on his ability to acquire both money and status. In short Lil's parents saw Weiss as the good provider they had always wanted for their only daughter.

Lil's parents occupied a house outside the city. It was pleasant to drive out there among the trees now covered in the russets and yellows of autumn. It was still warm enough, at the height of the day to sit in the garden with their pre-lunch drinks.

Lil's father was in fact a liberal host and the wine flowed throughout the afternoon. Lil's mother provided an excellent lunch and Weiss enjoyed a relaxed afternoon with his family.

As they drove home Weiss and Lil talked about their plans for a summer vacation trip. Weiss wanted to go to the lakes as usual. Lil was holding out for something a little more adventurous. By the time they had arrived home Weiss had all but given in to Lil and told her to get some information so they could make their bookings. Later that evening Ludovic and Lil lingered over a final glass before retiring to peaceful sleep.

By contrast this Monday morning dawned overcast and a chilly drizzle persisted throughout the morning.

No city on earth, however well regulated, has managed to arrange for the morning commute to be free of stress and delay. The tram lines in the centre of Weiss' city were under repair and the traffic crawled past the work site churning up a slurry of yellow brown mud. Joylessly Weiss joined the queue of cars that stop-started on its way into the city.

The Compliance Department occupied an office block in the central business district of the city. It was a landmark in its own right, rising several stark grey stories above the surrounding buildings and in the centre of an extensive tarmac area devoted to car parking for the Department's officials. The whole campus was protected by a high wire fence which was topped with razor wire.

Weiss turned into the campus, passing through the guarded entrance gates that swung open for him at the sight of the small, square blue badge attached to his windscreen. He gestured thanks to the guard in his booth who returned the greeting with a deferential salute.

The residue of Weiss' good humour, which he had managed to retain despite the traffic delays, ebbed away as he approached his parking space. Someone had already parked there.

Weiss drew up behind the trespasser and switched off his engine. The car in his space was new and shiny and unmarked by any sign that it had been driven through the muddy streets. Weiss ran his hand along its lustrous dark green paintwork. He was seething inwardly as he looked about in a vain attempt to spy out the owner.

There was no point in wreaking damage on the interloper although for a passing moment Weiss contemplated letting down a tyre or ripping off a colour coordinated windscreen wiper. The drizzling rain was finding its way under his collar, cooling his ire. This would have to be sorted out calmly and the culprit reprimanded coolly with sharply pointed and well considered words. Weiss got back into his car and drove out of the compound.

After circling the Compliance Department building and the surrounding streets for what seemed like an age Weiss found a parking space several blocks and some minutes soaking walk from the Department building.

He trudged back to his office. The rain continued to fall steadily and soaking as only chill drizzle can. When he finally reached his office his weekend mood had completely evaporated.

Else seemed to take a much too relaxed view of the incident for Weiss' liking. She would take care of it, she soothed. There had been a number of new starters at the Department. It was probably all a mistake on the part of one of the new people who hadn't been properly inducted into the Department's protocols.

How, Weiss asked, was it possible for even the most uninformed individual to make such a mistake. The fact of his entitlement, his exclusive entitlement, to that parking space was clearly indicated. There was an enamelled sign designating the spot as his own and pointing out his entitlement as a consequence of his rank. Only a blind man or someone of a defiant persuasion would thus usurp his position.

Privately, and he would never speak about this suspicion aloud, he wondered if this was some conspiracy to vex him. He speculated on the identity of the culprit. He asked himself who he had offended recently.

His jacket was still soaked from the drizzling rain. Else took it from him and hung it by a radiator. She could see from the set of his shoulders and the clench of his jaw that this minor inconvenience had stressed Weiss considerably. His face was the colour of beetroot and he clenched his fists spasmodically; a sure sign of inner tension which Else recognised all too well.

'Sit down and relax. You look like you are on the verge of a heart attack,' she ordered. 'Calm down and I'll get your coffee.'

'Sort out the parking space first. Don't bother with coffee'

'There's plenty of time. The whole day in fact. Here, just relax.'

Else stood behind him and reached over to massage Weiss' shoulders and the back of his neck. She chatted about his weekend, agreeing that Lil was right not to share his enjoyment of films noirs. Who was this Robert Mitchum anyway?

By the time she had finished Weiss' mood was undergoing a pleasant renaissance and he was ready for coffee. The only shred of irritation he now felt was due to the chill dampness of his trouser legs. He was ready for coffee and to leave the parking question to Else.

'You're coming tonight?' she queried on her way into the outer office.

It was a sign that the incident of the parking space had affected Weiss considerably that he found it necessary to ask 'Tonight?'

'Monday's our night. Monday and Wednesday. You always come round...for a couple of hours.'

Thus recalled to the normal flow of his life's routine Weiss agreed that he would be round at Else's apartment as was usual on a Monday evening. In fact he wouldn't miss it for anything.

'That's good. I'll make us something nice, 'Else concluded as she closed the door behind her.

Weiss pushed the morning's incident to the back of his mind and pulled the pile of papers from his in-tray towards him. He had nothing particular to do that day, no meetings scheduled and no assignments on hand. He had promised himself a quiet day just catching up on paperwork and routine.

He tried to work but despite Else's soothing and the coffee she brought him promptly, the incident of the parking space still rankled. He shuffled papers around his desk and three times he looked out of his window to see if the offending vehicle was still there. It was.

He sipped his coffee. Else had even brought some biscuits on a china plate. Weiss valued these little luxuries. Else hadn't just brought any biscuits; these were his particular favourites. He munched on one as he read over a document.

Weiss was a stickler for the protocols of the department. He was especially careful of anything that tended to reflect his own status or generated prestige for himself. He valued that parking space. It was a privilege. It was just like he valued this office, at the corner of the building with double aspect windows. His pictures were on the wall. Each carefully chosen and paid for by the department. He enjoyed sitting behind the big rosewood desk, another symbol of his status.

He picked up one or two of the objects that were lined up on his desk. The department liked to award staff with little crystal or plastic mementoes of significant achievements or of participation in high visibility projects. Weiss had seven or eight set out on one side of the desk. He was proud of them. He often fondled them as if they were his own children.

Weiss could be an especially difficult man to work for, it had to be admitted. Although Weiss if asked would say he rather saw himself more as someone who demanded excellence. Weiss didn't think of himself as vicious or a bully, like some of his colleague in his opinion. No, he simply demanded attention to detail and strict adherence to the procedural manual. Behind his back he was known as 'By the Book' Weiss and a collective howl of dismay was known to rise up from the lower floors when staff found themselves assigned to one of his investigations.

Those who sat in authority in the Compliance Department didn't seem to mind his approach though. He had been promoted several times and was often singled out for particular congratulation by the Director.

Else came in and cleared away the empty cup and plate. Weiss asked if she had sorted out the parking issue. He was not best pleased to know that she had not, as yet, made any progress. By way of mild admonition he asked for another coffee.

Then the phone rang. Weiss picked up and heard the familiar voice of the Director.

'Weiss, I need to see you.'

'Yes, Director. I'll come down straightaway.'

‘I’m not in my office. I want you to come to me.’ The Director gave a street address that Weiss did not recognise. He got out from behind his desk and checked the map of the city that hung on the opposite wall. The street was on the western edge of the city in an industrial district. Weiss had never been in that area.

‘Come now. And, Weiss, don’t tell anyone where you are going,’ the Director was continuing.

‘This seems to be highly irregular. Departmental directive…’

‘The directive does not apply in this case,’ the Director cut in. He seemed rather testy. ‘And don’t tell anyone that you are meeting me,’ he continued.

‘But…’

‘You have my authority, Weiss. That should be enough for you.’

‘Very well. I’ll come to you now.’

‘Don’t rush. Leave the office calmly. No fuss. We don’t want to arouse curiosity.’

‘No, Director. I may be a little time. I had to park in the street. Someone has parked in my space.’

‘I’m not interested in trivia, Weiss. Just get on your way.’

'Yes Director. Trivial I agree. I should be about thirty minutes'

The Director hung up and Weiss listened to the angry wasp-buzzing of the dial-tone for a few seconds, speculating on this strange turn of events. Clandestine meetings were not the stuff of daily business in the Compliance Department.

Weiss recovered himself and replaced his own receiver. He recovered his jacket. It was still wretchedly damp but he shrugged himself into it. Else came in with coffee as he hurried past her.

'Where are you going? Don't you want your coffee?'

'I need to go out.'

'Was it that phone call?'

'Can't say.'

'But why the hurry? Where are you going?'

'I can't say'

'This is very irregular. What do I say if anyone needs you?'

'You'll just have to say you don't know.'

'Why can't you tell me?'

'Need to know. It's on a need to know basis.'

'And I don't need to know? Can I know when you might be back?'

'I don't know. Really. I have no idea.'

'Tonight then?'

'Yes. Yes, of course.'

'Call me if...Well call me'

'Yes, of course.'

As he took the stairs down to the ground floor two at a time Weiss speculated that he had singularly failed to avert any curiosity on Else's part. As he stepped out in the rain he could imagine her conversation at lunch break with the other secretaries. His behaviour was completely at odds with the usual tenor of affairs in the Compliance Dept.

There had been no let-up in the volume of traffic and it took Weiss nearly an hour to reach the location that he'd been given by the Director. As expected the area was run down, scarred by the remnants of heavy industry and acned by dilapidated housing set in terraces. There was no sign of life on the streets.

Weiss looked around for a place that the Director would have been likely to have chosen for a discreet meeting. He was certain that he had found the right area; the Director had told him to come to a particular corner on a cross-road in the centre of the district. Looking around, however, Weiss could see only a church. The land on the other corners was covered in weeds and the rubble from the buildings that had formerly stood there. This church was the only option.

In the city churches were an uncommon sight. Some, of course, of the most striking and lavishly decorated examples had been kept to attract and please foreign tourists. Yet others were now museums and some of the more modern had been converted to social uses. All of these, however, were located in the central districts. This church was not modern but a throwback to medieval times, with a steeple and faux battlements. It stood like a derelict awaiting the ship-breakers amid a sea of wasteland.

Weiss climbed the worn down steps and pushed on the thick wooden door. It gave easily and opened without a sound, He went in. The place smelt of religion, that musty smell of candle grease and dust and decaying books. There was a priest at the altar; all dressed up like a black crow. There was an old woman too, polishing the floor. He looked about for the Director but there was no-one else visible. A row of confessional boxes stood along one wall. Weiss checked each one. No one.

The priest seemed to finish whatever task had been occupying him and disappeared into an inner room. He emerged a few minutes later now gorgeously dressed in a brilliantly coloured robe over his black garments. He rang a small bell and the old woman scuttled to a seat at the front of the church just below the ornate pulpit that seemed to soar above the pews.Weiss heard the doors open and shuffling feet approaching. He turned to look at the newcomers expecting to see the Director. Instead a small group of soberly dressed men and women, maybe five in total, had entered the church. Weiss watched them as they each found a preferred spot among the pews and settled themselves. The priest began to chant in a high nasal voice and the congregation, such as it was, stood to respond.

Weiss took a seat at the back of the church. He was wondering where in the desolation outside this collection of religious devotees had sprung from when he felt a hand brush his shoulder. It was the Director who had seemingly, himself, sprung from nowhere. He motioned for Weiss to follow him.

They went into a side chapel decorated with the statue of the saint to which it had been dedicated. Weiss noticed the bare feet of the saint were standing on the pincers and other tools which were doubtless symbols of the method of her martyrdom. A large wooden cross bearing the tormented body of a Christ figure loomed over the space. The Director motioned for Weiss to sit and sat alongside him. Weiss felt a momentary discomfort at the closeness of the bulk of his superior. He could smell an odour of earthiness about the man.

The Director was speaking in a subdued tone as the religious service droned a background motif.

'Weiss, I am relying on your discretion and your good sense. I have an assignment for you which will call for resourceful and discreet handling.'

'This is very irregular...' Weiss began but the Director laid a hand on his arm and cut him short.

'Just be quiet and listen to what I have to tell you. If time permits you can ask questions when I've finished. Do you understand?'

Weiss nodded agreement and the Director continued:

'Here is a file. Show it to no-one else. It contains highly confidential information.' A file had appeared in the Directors hand, produced from within the folds of his thick winter coat.

Weiss fought down strong feelings of misgiving and forced himself to stay silent. This was not how things were done in the Compliance Department. A committee would be formed. A method of investigation debated and adopted. A team assembled. Weiss began to regret even coming to this meeting. But then how do you decline an instruction from the Director?

'Take it then,' the Director thrust the red jacketed file at Weiss who despite his reservations automatically reached out and took it. 'Well, conceal it. Put it out of sight.'

Weiss wished that he had worn a coat or brought along a briefcase. All of this had wrong-footed him. He pushed the file inside his still damp jacket, nestling it in his armpit. The director was continuing to speak:

'Take it away and read it carefully but make sure no-one else sees it in your hands or overlooks you. In the course of this investigation you will report directly to me. No-one else is to be involved.'

'I'm to work alone?' Weiss couldn't help himself.

'That is what I am saying. When you have read the file make contact with the parties mentioned in it. They have no suspicion that we – the Department – have this information. Tell them that your inspection is strictly routine. Part of a new programme. Of course they'll cooperate – they have no choice. But then they'll make sure that you see nothing you shouldn't. Make sure you get to them today. Speed is critical, catch them off guard'

Weiss held his tongue and looked blankly at the Director.

'I can see you are uncomfortable with this. Clandestine arrangements aren't usual but in this case…The fact is everything in that file has come from a source inside the company you are to investigate. That's where the need for discretion arises.'

'A whistle-blower? Is he in the file?'

'Yes, a whistle-blower. However, he remains anonymous. We cannot risk exposing him or her.'

'But…'

'The person will contact you…as necessary. You'll be guided. Trust me.'

Weiss was silent. He had no choice but to trust the Director. He had no choice in following his superiors instructions however suspect the approach might seem.

'Questions?'

'It's against departmental regulations for a confidential file to be kept outside the secure room at the department.'

'That's not a question.'

'I'm not sure that I should be doing this.'

'Weiss – I've already said that you have to trust me on this. Come on now – we've been colleagues for how long? I am giving you authority to contravene the regulation. That should be enough. Any more thoughts?'

Weiss shook his head.

'Good. Then go. You leave first.'

Bewildered, Ludovic Weiss stood at the foot of the church steps in a state of complete confusion. He had literally been ordered out of his comfort zone and he didn't know what was actually expected of him. He was not a spy or yet a policeman. He was a lawyer by education. A civil servant by employment and while he was charged with enforcing the statutes of the state this was always as part of an investigating team, with proper sanction and authority. Now he was being told to trust his superior and act on his own initiative albeit in a discreet and covert way. He was not even sure that what he was being told to do was strictly legal in itself.

How does one question the direction of a senior figure? Weiss realised with a shudder that he had no reference point. There was no-one to ask, no-one to tell. He felt a pang of envy for the whistle-blower.

Weiss' stomach felt empty. He suspected it was all due to the inner turmoil brought on by the day's events. On further consideration he realised that he hadn't eaten since breakfast. He had even missed his second cup of morning coffee.

Just down the street he saw what looked like a lighted sign. On closer inspection he was pleased to see it was attached to a small but cosy looking café quite at odds with the surrounding desolation.

When he entered the place was empty except for the owner behind the bar counter and a waitress engaged in laying cutlery on the tables. He noticed a couple of booths towards the back of the room, out of sight of the road outside and not overlooked from any angle. He slid into the rear most booth, hunkering into a corner as if to ensure invisibility. The waitress came by and without directly looking at her, Weiss ordered a glass of beer and a sandwich.

When she went away he eased the file from beneath his jacket. He flinched at the sight of its bright red jacket that seemed to scream to the outside world demanding that everyone look at it. He edged it onto his knees beneath the level of the table. From a brief glance he could make out that the file contained hand written letters, some computer printouts and various photocopied pages of figures.

Weiss became absorbed in leafing through the papers and nearly jumped out of his skin when the waitress returned. He thrust the file further under the table but the girl barely seemed to notice as she slid his glass of beer and a plate across to him.

When she had gone Weiss brought the file back out onto the table. He cast a surreptitious glance around the room and bent to the papers again. Fortunately someone had thought to prepare a summary of the contents and the salient facts and placed it in the front of the file. From this Weiss gathered that the trading firm in question had been guilty of many violations over the years, all of which they had been successful in hiding from the authorities of the state.

The café door opened again just as Weiss came to the end of the summary. There was a quiet murmur of voices, like a soft wind stirring grasses and the congregation from the church spread themselves around the room. Weiss decided it was time to go and slipped the file back under his jacket. He would only be safe to read the thing thoroughly at home. Now, however, he had to set up the meeting with the offenders. Yes, Weiss had decided that that was how he should think of them. He would have to meet with the offenders with only the sketchy knowledge afforded by the summary. Probably not a bad thing he thought. With scant knowledge there wasn't much he could give away during the meeting. All in all both he and the offenders would probably be equally mystified by what was happening.

Weiss got back to his car, thankful at least that the rain had stopped and watery sunshine had replaced it. Holding the file open on his lap he telephoned to the company noted on the front sheet and asked to speak to the managing director. He was amazed to find that his call was put straight through and that the voice that answered was actually the managing director and not a secretary set on knowing the reason for the call and on denying him access to her boss. He was equally shocked by the reaction to his request for a meeting.

'Ah yes, of course. Whenever you like. This afternoon about three o' clock? Would that suit you? We have been expecting your call.'

Weiss stammered his agreement, hung up and slumped back in his seat. He noticed that a thin film of cold sweat had formed on his forehead. He had braced himself for...what exactly? A blank refusal to see him? Prevarication? Demands to explain, in detail, his reasons for the actual impertinence of asking for a meeting? All of these were variously the usual preliminaries to a planned inspection by the Compliance Department. By contrast this had felt like pushing on the proverbial open door.

Weiss realised that he had little time to get to the premises of the trading company, InterTrade, he was to investigate by the time agreed for the meeting. He dumped the file on the passenger seat and set of in a squeal of tyres.

The premises of InterTrade looked perfectly normal. Trucks were pulled up alongside concrete piers that jutted from a long shed which itself was attached to a three floor office block. A pair of trucks was drawn up with engines idling, waiting to take their place when one of the loading dock piers became free. Weiss pulled into the parking spot designated for visitors that was positioned handily by the front entrance to the office block. What was he supposed to do with this file? It lay like a pile of toxic material on the passenger seat. It was threatening and made Weiss feel distinctly uncomfortable every time he glanced at it. He wanted it out of his sight. But where? He didn't have a coat or blanket to cover it. He didn't have a briefcase in which to hide it. He thought about locking it in the boot of the car, but cars can be stolen. He looked around the carpark. Was anyone watching? The actual possession of this damned sheaf of papers in a flimsy cardboard jacket was making him paranoid.

He couldn't sit there all day and the clock on the dashboard was already ticking down to the time set for the meeting. Weiss grabbed the file and holding it close to his chest burst through the front door.

He was expected. A security badge made out in his name was already on the reception desk. A young woman hovered by the inner door ready to conduct him to the meeting room.

'I'm sorry,' Weiss began, 'I came out in a bit of a rush. Could you let me have a pad of paper – A4 would be good. In fact two would be very helpful.'

The receptionist handed the requested stationery to Weiss and treated him to a sympathetic smile and asked if he needed anything else. Weiss sandwiched the file between the two blocks of paper. It didn't actually disguise the file but at least, Weiss felt, it was not so much in evidence. Thus calmed Weiss followed the young woman along a corridor and into the conference room.

The managing director who sat at the head of the long, rose wood, meeting table, greeted Weiss affably and invited him to take a seat at his right hand. Water, coffee, juice were all offered and as if on cue half a dozen men and one woman entered the room and took their seats around the table. Introductions were made.

Each and every one of the people around the table appeared bland to Weiss. So bland in fact as to be faceless and, Weiss conjectured, would be unrecognisable outside of the room which gave them a context.

Although unprepared it was straightforward enough for Weiss to set out his requirements for his forthcoming inspection. It was, though, with some relief that he realised that no-one in the room demurred at any of his requests. The faceless group bent over their own notepads and assiduously recorded his every request. It was as though the whole of their operation was an open book and all Weiss needed was to ask to be shown their innermost corporate secrets. Weiss thought cynically that although this was a comfortable beginning, this would change radically when he got too close to some real evidence of wrongdoing.

It was agreed that Weiss would start his inspection on the Wednesday, giving a day's grace for the InterTrade management to gather the initial materials that Weiss had specified. In just over an hour Weiss found himself back in his car, still clutching the file sandwiched between the paper pads to his chest. He speculated on who in the building in front of him might be the anonymous informant and how or when this person might make contact with him. Could it have been one of the faceless group around the conference table? The woman maybe? He sensed, rather than saw a movement outside the car.

One of the faceless ones, a man, had stepped out of the front door and was standing just looking at Weiss. He made no movement when Weiss caught sight of him. He just stood there. Weiss wound down the window and was about to speak when the grey suited man slipped ghostlike back into the building. Weiss wound up the window and drove off.

It was too late to go back to the office. It was already getting dark and Weiss did not feel up to finding a parking space in the street and walking in the still damp evening air back to the building. Instead he drove around trying to make sense of the day and killing time until he could be sure that Else would be home. He needed to talk about this with someone and Else could be trusted to listen even if his story had to be edited to remove the sensitive parts.

Weiss reached Else's flat and sat in the car for a while before climbing the steps up to the second floor apartment. The front of the place was in darkness, no lights in the hallway and none behind the curtained windows of the lounge. Weiss rang the bell and heard the chimes echo in the empty hallway.

No-one came. Weiss stood looking at the door for several minutes before he rang the bell again. Still no sign of life. He speculated briefly that Else might have been kept late at the office. But then she could always have called him. He checked his phone; no message, no missed calls.

Weiss took a walk along the balcony that lead past the other flats on the second floor. At the end he turned back and caught sight of the block warden watching him across the space that separated Else's block from its twin. He returned to Else's apartment and rang again. He peaked through the letterbox into the darkness. No lights showed from the rooms at the rear of the apartment. He checked his watch. He had been there for fifteen minutes already.

He took out his phone and dialled Else's number. He listened to the ringing in his earpiece and the ringing from within the flat. Nobody picked up. He rang Else's mobile number and listened as the recorded voice of the message service cut in straightaway. For a second he considered leaving a message and then cut the call.

Standing there in the chill night air he was struck by the ridiculous nature of his situation. He had a delightful wife and he knew that he loved Lil. He had a pleasant home, comfortable and welcoming. Yet here he was waiting for, not only his mistress but his secretary to let him in for a couple of hours of illicit... what? Pleasure? Intimacy? He was forced to laugh at himself although he suppressed the impulsion to do so out loud.

He felt someone watching him and turned to see the block warden was now standing at the corner of the balcony, by the steps he had mounted from the parking space. Weiss tried the bell one last time without any hope of an answer. He knew he risked arousing the interest of the warden if he continued to loiter at the doorway. Questions would be asked, names recorded. An inconvenience which might lead to a need for explanations. Best not to provoke it.

Weiss brushed past the warden as he made for the stairs. He descended quickly hoping that he had not made himself too memorable. He reassured himself that Else, when she returned from whatever was keeping her, would be able to explain his presence should the warden prove curious.

He paused at the door of his car and looked up towards Else's flat. He was surprised and not a little annoyed to see a light go on behind the lounge curtains. He debated the idea of returning now that he knew there was someone definitely in the flat. Was that someone in fact Else? Was there a visitor? Someone of whom he was unaware?

The file was on the front seat. He had neglected it in his desire to see Else and unburden himself. A foolhardy move. He realised that now. Was Else as trustworthy as he had assumed?

Weiss dismissed these unwelcome thoughts and told himself that tonight he needed to focus on the assignment and to try to unravel the unsettling events of the last few hours. It was already late. He needed to get home and read the file thoroughly. Tomorrow, he told himself, he would confront the Director when he made his initial report.

It was very late by the time that Weiss reached his own apartment. Lil was already in bed, fast asleep, curled in a foetal ball beneath the duvet. Weiss sat in the darkened lounge with a single table light to read by. He had poured himself a glass of scotch whiskey and opened the troublesome file on his lap. He leafed through the contents and then read carefully and with attention for a couple of hours. The nature of the offenses was quite clearly spelled out and the evidence so far accumulated made a damning case. Weiss began to wonder what more his own investigation was supposed to unearth.

Eventually Weiss found his attention wandering and his head drooped over the file. If he was to be at all effective the next day he must try to get some sleep in the few hours that remained of the night. The question of what to do with the file again bubbled to the surface. After some thought Weiss decided that it would be safe enough locked in his briefcase which he slid under the bed.

Thus assured Weiss climbed under the covers. He put his arm around Lil. She stirred briefly, uttered a soft sigh and was instantly again wrapped in a deep sleep.

Printed in Poland
by Amazon Fulfillment
Poland Sp. z o.o., Wrocław

59307243R00110